*"Who are* you?*"*

For the briefest of moments, their gazes wed.

Dante's eyes glinted as if he knew exactly what Elle looked like stark naked...and he approved. The intimate suggestion in his stare caused her to catch her breath.

Nature had packaged him in a hard muscular frame. Then Elle spied something that completely rattled her. There, at his wrist, circled the hint of dark blue ink.

A tattoo. Talk about out of place.

Who was he *really?*

The look that passed between them was weighted with a meaning Elle couldn't begin to unravel. Her cheeks tingled. How embarrassing— she was blushing!

What was happening to her? One minute she'd been minding her own business, and the next minute this sharply dressed, broad-shouldered stranger had her locked in some kind of sensual hold.

She didn't trust a man who could make her feel so aroused with just a look.

Or could she?

*Blaze*™

Dear Reader,

Welcome to Confidential Rejuvenations, a swanky boutique hospital in Austin, Texas, providing first-class, hush-hush health care to celebrities, VIPS and legendary luminaries. Their philosophy—you do it, we keep it strictly confidential.

But all is not as it seems at this lavish, spa-style treatment facility, because inside, it's a hotbed of lust, cover-ups, secrets and lies.

I'm really excited about my new series PERFECT ANATOMY, featuring three best friends who keep the titillating secrets of their exclusive clientele while desperately hiding a few skeletons of their own. Smart, sassy, accomplished, these women can skillfully navigate both the human body and the glitzy world of their high-profile patients. Save your life? You betcha. Discreet? No doubt. Sexy? As hell. Play hard after a tough day on the job? Where do you think they get their secrets?

And when they fall in love, they pull out all the stops.

I hope you enjoy the new series, where I get to put my twenty years of nursing experience to good use.

Much love,

*Lori Wilde*

# CROSSING THE LINE
## Lori Wilde

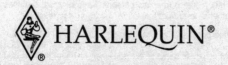

HARLEQUIN®

TORONTO • NEW YORK • LONDON
AMSTERDAM • PARIS • SYDNEY • HAMBURG
STOCKHOLM • ATHENS • TOKYO • MILAN • MADRID
PRAGUE • WARSAW • BUDAPEST • AUCKLAND

ISBN-13: 978-0-373-79403-4
ISBN-10:    0-373-79403-7

CROSSING THE LINE

## ABOUT THE AUTHOR

Lori Wilde is the author of forty books. She's been nominated for a RITA® Award and four *Romantic Times BOOKreviews* Reviewers' Choice Awards. Her books have been excerpted in *Cosmopolitan*, *Redbook* and *Quick & Simple*. Lori teaches writing online through Ed2go. She's an R.N. trained in forensics, and she volunteers at a battered women's shelter.

## Books by Lori Wilde

### HARLEQUIN BLAZE

Don't miss any of our special offers. Write to us at the following address for information on our newest releases.

Harlequin Reader Service
U.S.: 3010 Walden Ave., P.O. Box 1325, Buffalo, NY 14269
Canadian: P.O. Box 609, Fort Erie, Ont. L2A 5X3

To Candy Halliday—dear friend and medical cohort. Keep writing, Candy. The world needs more of your unique perspective.

## 1

FROM ITS STATELY EXTERIOR overlooking the bucolic Colorado River just outside Austin, Texas, Confidential Rejuvenations—a small but criminally expensive medical treatment facility for the crème-de-la-crème—exuded an atmosphere of supreme tranquility.

The lush green lawns were perfectly clipped, as were the bountiful privacy hedges. Ivy-twined trellises shaded genteel redwood park benches. The profusion of petunias, pansies, daisies and daffodils in full bloom undulated in the breeze, testifying to the exemplary gardening skills of the groundskeepers.

A luxurious flagstone walkway led toward the discrete front entrance in one direction. The other fork wound its way to an elaborate hand-carved gazebo positioned on a bluff above the sensuous curve of the river.

Confidential Rejuvenations was a favorite recuperation spot for southwest politicians, actors, musicians and other VIPs seeking various cures for addictions, aging and crisis of identity.

But Dr. Dante Nash wasn't fooled by appearances.

Beneath the serene surface, behind the healing promises made in the glossy full-color, trifold brochure resting on the passenger seat beside him, beyond those stately vine-covered walls, lurked a shadowy menace.

Careers lay on the line. Fortunes stood to be lost or gained. Lives hung in the balance.

And Dante was the catalyst. Sent undercover by the FBI to find out exactly who at Confidential Rejuvenations was trafficking in a very potent sex drug.

The designer party drug, street named Rapture, had been popping up on the club scene and college campuses around the Southwest for the past several months. It was being blamed for a dozen senseless deaths, and the FBI had traced the genesis of the substance to this quaint boutique hospital, partially owned by Dante's former college roommate, Dr. Mark Lawson.

For the past three years, Dante had worked for the Bureau as a plastic surgeon, giving new faces to people entering the Witness Protection Program. This was his first actual undercover assignment; he'd been hand selected for the project due to both his skills as a surgeon and his connection to Mark.

Dante didn't know if his ex-roommate was involved or not, but if Lawson was, he would take the man down without a moment's hesitation. Nothing was going to stop Dante from getting those drugs off the street. Ultimately, he was doing this to avenge Leeza's death.

He winced at the thought of his murdered sister. Of all the things they had suffered together. Sense memories of his miserable childhood rolled over him. The stench of sour mash whiskey on his father's breath. The feel of a leather strap slapping against his skin. The taste of fear on his tongue. He thought of the beatings he'd taken. Both from neighborhood thugs and his old man, until he had learned to fight back, learned how to protect his baby sister.

Painfully he recalled the way Leeza had looked the last time he'd seen her, strung out on drugs, eyes red, unwashed hair matted to her head, track marks running up and down her arms as she carried that hopeless, helpless air of the damned.

He'd tried to help her. Had gotten her into rehab twice, and she'd run away both times, unable to resist the seductive allure of heroin and the dangerous pull of her mob-connected boyfriend, Furio Gambezi.

Dante's desire to save his sister was the motivating factor in his decision to join the FBI after he'd completed his residency in reconstructive cosmetic surgery. It was the burning need to see justice served. His hunger to even the score.

Patience.

His body tensed, fingers tightening around the leather steering wheel, his mind on full alert.

Dante stopped the Porsche Carrera GT—the FBI had provided it as a prop—at the security guard station and rolled down the window. The car had been seized during a drug bust. After the mobster who'd owned it had gone to prison, the FBI had been allowed to keep it for use in undercover operations such as this one.

He had to admit he took some satisfaction in driving one of the world's most expensive sports cars, especially since it had been confiscated from a gangster. The sensuous purr of the engine, the luxurious feel of the butter-soft leather, the illicit thrill. It put him in mind of truly great sex.

Unfortunately, it had been so long since he'd *had* truly great sex he was a bit fuzzy on the details of exactly how good it did feel. His job didn't allow much time for developing intimate contacts and he'd never been proud of his brief, meaningless affairs.

"Morning, sir," the security guard on duty greeted him.

"Good morning."

"You here to visit?" The guard eyed him. "Or are you a patient checking in for treatment?"

Dante wore high-end sunglasses and a dove-gray silk Armani suit. His cologne was exotic, his hair fashionably clipped and his fingernails manicured to a high sheen. A purple orchid boutonniere nestled in the buttonhole of his outrageously priced suit.

Nothing about the slick exterior represented the real Dante. His inner soul was much darker, much grittier, much more tortured than the glitzy image he projected. He was playing the part of an upscale young plastic surgeon with an ego bigger than God. It was his duty to embody the role. Insecurities and vulnerabilities had no place in this plan. Nor was there any room for mistakes.

"I'm the new physician, Dr. Dante Nash," he said with an air of aloof entitlement, and presented the man his driver's license.

The security guard checked Dante's credentials against a list on his clipboard. "Ah, yes, here you are. Welcome to Confidential Rejuvenations, Dr. Nash."

"Thank you." Dante glanced at the man's name badge. He might have to play the arrogant, rich doctor, but he could still be civil. "Freddie."

"Have a nice day, sir."

"You do so as well."

The guard pressed a button that opened the wrought-iron gate onto a red cobblestone driveway. Dante followed the road around more privacy hedges and white rock retaining walls. The breeze was cooler up here in the hills than it was in Austin. He kept the window rolled down and flipped off the air conditioner. The fresh smell of spring floated into the car.

Leeza had died in the spring and he hated the season for it. Dante clenched his teeth.

Three years had gone by since her death, but he was still having trouble letting go of his anger. Still haunted by the fact he'd been unable to save her.

*Don't think about Leeza. Not now.*

A quaint, hand-carved wooden sign directed him to the physicians' parking area. He parked the Porsche, rolled up the windows and got out. A punch of a button on the keypad locked the doors and activated the alarm.

Another sign along the sidewalk pointed to the private entrance to the emergency department open exclusively to Confidential Rejuvenation's elite clientele. It was closer than walking around to the front entrance so he went in that way. Stepping through the pneumatic doors, he walked into the plushiest emergency waiting room he'd ever seen.

The place was spotless. The couches and chairs were made of sage-colored leather and looked brand-new. The televisions mounted on the walls were all forty-two-inch plasma screens and came equipped with TiVo. They were turned on and playing to an empty room.

The potted ficus tree was real and the complimentary coffee was gourmet. Polished metal on the fleet of well-maintained wheelchairs stowed along the far wall gleamed brightly underneath the recessed lighting.

Even more impressive was what was missing.

No gory blood stains. No suffering moans. No acrid smell of gunshot residue. No distraught family members sobbing their hearts out.

No question why it was so damned clean. Clearly emergency medicine wasn't a specialty of Confidential Rejuvenations.

He paused to take it all in.

There had to be a reception desk around here somewhere. The thick double doors before him were locked. A sign instructed visitors to ring the bell for service. Dante glanced up and spied the small, discreet surveillance cameras mounted at all four corners of the entryway.

He was being watched.

Dante pressed the button. A pleasant disembodied voice greeted him. He identified himself. A buzzer sounded and the doors swung open.

More signs.

Lab and Radiology and Surgery to the right. Admin and the cafeteria lay straight ahead. The actual emergency exam rooms themselves were to the left.

And not a single soul in sight.

Weird.

He was beginning to regret not walking around to the front entrance. This whole place was spooky as hell. Where did they keep the woman who'd buzzed him in?

Maybe it wasn't a real woman at all, he thought, but a robotic recording.

Suddenly, feeling as if he'd wandered onto a movie set of *Stepford Hospital,* he had a compelling urge to find a living human being. Pushed along by his anxiety, Dante turned left, rounded the corner and walked into a nightmare.

The reception area he'd been searching for was in utter chaos. Papers were strewn across the room, equipment knocked over, glass broken. Three sobbing nurses sat huddled on the floor behind the desk. Two people in street clothes lay bleeding profusely on the white tile floor. One of them was an elderly woman.

Like a splash of cold water doused in his face, shock was the first thing that hit Dante. It was quickly followed by a jolt of adrenaline. The air around him seemed to turn stale, heavy. His blood pounded sluggishly in his ears.

Another nurse, this one with a calm, brave expression on her face, was talking softly to a wild-eyed young man wearing a patient gown and pajama bottoms spattered with blood. Torn cotton restraints dangled from his wrists like extra appendages.

The man stood between the soft-spoken nurse and the huddled women. In his hand, he clutched a bloody bowie knife.

Even in the midst of the crisis, there was something about the nurse that commanded Dante's attention. She looked so…*earnest*—in a job that quickly made cynics of most—like a new graduate clinging to her ideal that healing the sick was the highest of callings.

Dante envied her.

And simultaneously lusted after her.

The lust surprised him. The feeling was so completely out of context and it had been such a very long time since he'd felt anything akin to this sudden need.

What the hell was wrong with him?

"Please, put the knife down. We can work this out. I know you really don't want to hurt anyone," the nurse cajoled.

"Stay back or I'll kill them all," the deranged patient threatened, his voice high and reedy.

Anger seized Dante then. Furrowed his brow, tightened the corners of his mouth and narrowed his eyes. He had been caught in the grip of this feeling many times. It was an old but dangerous friend.

Like the trained FBI agent he was, he sprang into action without hesitation. In two long-legged strides he was across the room, slapping one hand around the man's wrist and spinning him backward.

The red-haired nurse was screaming at him, but he was so intent on the task at hand that he couldn't process what she was saying.

Blow his cover or not, he would not allow this scumbag to harm another soul.

Determination, fear, anger, excitement slid thickly through his veins, rolling, crashing, thundering. Dante hooked the crook of his elbow around the assailant's neck and squeezed tight.

*Surrender the knife, you bastard, or die.*

ONE MINUTE ELLE KINGSTON, RN, and her emergency room nursing staff were role-playing a hostage standoff scenario, and the next minute, this sharp-dressed, broad-shouldered stranger had her orderly—who was portraying the hostage-taker—gripped in a deadly chokehold.

The orderly made a strangling noise. His face was red, his eyes bulging. His fingers loosened and he dropped the rubber bowie knife smeared with a theatrical solution simulating blood. The knife bounced harmlessly against the tile.

"What in the hell do you think you're doing?" Elle demanded of the stranger, her body shot full of fear. "Let go of Ricky before you kill him."

The stranger's gaze pierced her so thoroughly she felt a breath-stealing blur of heated intensity.

"It's a drill." Elle glowered and laid her hands on her hips. "You're suffocating my orderly."

"Oh." His shoulders lowered, and for the briefest of moments the stranger looked sheepish.

He let Ricky go.

The orderly bolted across the room, hand to his neck. "Not cool, dude," he croaked. "Not cool."

The nurses behind the desk rose to their feet, dusting off the seats of their scrubs pants. The two "bodies" on the floor sat up. One was the E.D. front desk ward secretary, sixty-eight-year-old Maxine Woodbury, who loved Confidential Rejuvenations so much she ignored the fact that she was past retirement age and just kept on working.

The second "murder victim" was the affable hospital janitor, Carlisle Jones. Carlisle was the father of five, and he frequently moonlighted as an extra in Austin-based movies and television commercials. He'd appeared in three of Sandra Bullock's films and was on a first-name basis with Matthew McConaughey. Carlisle was always up for a starring role in Elle's disaster-preparedness plans.

Everyone eyed the stranger speculatively.

"I didn't realize it was a drill," he muttered.

"So you think you're what?" Elle folded her arms over her chest and assessed him with a glare. "The Armani Avenger?"

He cracked a smile, albeit a brief one. "I subdued the attacker."

"You caught him by surprise. Do you know how irresponsible that was? Ever heard the adage that a gentle word turns away wrath? If Ricky had been a real patient and the nurses real hostages…" Elle shook her head.

The stranger put a hand to the left side of his chest. It was a quick, slight gesture, barely noticeable. But Elle, who had grown up the daughter, sister, granddaughter and niece of cops, had the strangest feeling he was wearing a shoulder holster underneath that fancy, dove-gray pin-stripped silk suit. It was a gesture that said if the hostage situation had been real, he would have shot the suspect.

But her instincts about him and the image he projected didn't fit.

Oh, the man looked like he could be a cop—he possessed the right posture, the right air of self-assurance, the "no bullshit" eyes. Like he'd seen too much of the world, knew too much to ever really trust anyone again.

What didn't jive were the suit and the hair and the platinum watch and the way he seemed to be biting his tongue to keep from saying what was really on his mind.

She hated to admit it, but he intrigued her.

Plus, he was exceptionally handsome. Not that she let good looks sway her opinion of someone.

He leaned toward her, narrowing the gap between them. His gaze was level and she felt it again.

Something oddly exciting.

The chemistry surged up. A rush of hormones that told her sex with this man would be very good indeed. She experienced the knowledge in her lungs, in the pit of her stomach, between her legs.

It was more than his coal-black, stylishly cut hair. More than the tawny eyes and the angular bow-shaped lips she was already imagining grazing softly across the nape of her neck. More than the sexy cleft in his hard, masculine chin. Nervously she raised a hand to her hairline and averted her eyes from his face.

He felt it, too.

She saw it in the almost imperceptible quickening of the pulse at the hollow of his throat. Elle flicked her gaze back to his.

His eyes narrowed, but his pupils widened. He was struggling for control, trying to recover without her noticing he'd been affected, trying to hide that he was interested.

Very interested.

"My goal was to defuse the situation as quickly as possible," he said, finally answering the question she'd posed. "Ever hear the adage that actions speak louder than words?"

He was throwing her words back at her. Giving as good as he got. Cop talk. He sounded like her parents and her brothers and her grandfather and her uncles.

"Do you always act first and ask questions later?"

"If need be."

"Seems like a dangerous way to live." She raised an eyebrow. It was almost as if he knew she'd pegged him. A cop trying to slip into someone else's skin. Was he undercover? But why would there be an undercover cop at Confidential Rejuvenations? Could it have anything to do with the series of unfortunate events that had been going on at the hospital?

Nah, she was jumping to conclusions, reading something into his behavior that wasn't there. Probably he was just like her—raised around policemen and steeped so long in the culture of law enforcement he behaved like a cop even when he wasn't one.

"A flaw of mine."

Now that definitely wasn't coplike, readily admitting a shortcoming. But she found it appealing. Mark had never once admitted he was wrong, not even when she'd caught him red-handed with Cassandra. Her ex-husband had tried to turn it around, make his cheating Elle's fault by saying she'd been too absorbed with her work.

The jackass.

"And," the stranger continued. "I apologize for disturbing your drill."

Admitting a fault *and* apologizing for it? From an alpha guy like this? She didn't buy it. He was trying too hard to make her like him.

Why?

"Who are you?" She cocked her head upward and crossed her arms over her chest again.

"Dante," a voice from behind Elle boomed. "You made it!"

Elle didn't have to turn to see who was speaking. She'd spent five years of her life listening to that voice. A voice that had made promises he never intended on keeping.

The voice of her rat bastard ex-husband, Mark Lawson.

Elle gritted her teeth and tried to tamp down her resentment. A year ago, just when she thought Mark was finally ready to start a family, after she had put him through medical school, worked double shifts while he completed his residency in psychiatrics, he had dumped her for one of his patients. A twenty-one-year-old actress named Cassandra Roberts.

Cassandra, bless her little heart, couldn't act her way out of a paper bag. But she was blond, beautiful and one shade above anorexic. Plus, her daddy was a big-wheel movie exec, and Mark had always been enamored of money, glitz and glamour.

Mark moved around Elle as if she didn't exist and clasped the stranger in a bear hug. "Dante, man, you look great."

So this was Dante Nash. Mark's college roommate, and the newest surgeon to join the staff of Confidential Rejuvenations.

Just her luck.

Back when she and Mark were married and he would occasionally get drunk and chatty, he would reminisce about his college days at the University of Texas. During those times he'd tell of the antics he and Dante had gotten into, recounting tales of their prowess on the football field.

And in the bedrooms of sorority houses.

According to Mark, Dante was something of a player. This explained the suit and the haircut and the Rolex and the brooding charm. Elle lumped him into the same category with her ex-husband.

Untrustworthy skeeve.

In her book, anyone who was a friend of Mark's was an enemy of hers.

*Now, Elle,* chided her good-girl side. *You only diminish yourself when you think like that. Not giving Mark power over your feelings is the best revenge. No need cluttering your mind with negativity.*

Maybe so, but it didn't seem as satisfying as the fantasy of slashing the tires on Mark's new Mercedes. She was still driving the compact Chevy she'd bought after she graduated from college ten long years ago.

Thank heavens for her two best friends, Vanessa and Julie. They also worked with her at Confidential Rejuvenations. In an attempt to deal with the stress of their professions and the secrets that the job forced them to keep, they'd formed an after-hours club where they could get together and vent. Sharing their hopes, dreams and fantasies with one another.

Her friends had been there for Elle during her divorce and they understood her even when her own family didn't. The group was meeting on Wednesday night and she couldn't wait to tell them what had happened in the E.D. with the new surgeon.

Her family thought she was crazy for staying at Confidential Rejuvenations, considering she had to see Mark on a daily basis. She would admit it was particularly difficult when Cassandra Roberts showed up, dangling adoringly from his arm.

But this was the best job Elle had ever had. For one

thing, she was extremely well paid. She couldn't go anywhere else and make the same kind of money. Plus, she was given lots of autonomy and she adored the staff. The VIP patients could be challenging at times, simply because they were VIPs, but Elle enjoyed taking care of people. Being a caregiver, however, had its drawbacks. For instance it prevented you from making a voodoo doll of your ex-husband and sticking sharp pointy things through it.

"Come on, let me show you to your office," Mark said. Without even bothering to introduce the new doctor to the staff, he slung an arm around Dante's shoulder and propelled him toward the door.

Typical Mark. No thought for anyone except himself.

As her ex-husband dragged the new physician past her, Dante's elbow accidentally grazed Elle's breast.

Sharply she inhaled as the shock of the unintentional contact spread out through her nerve endings.

She saw Dante glance down at her from his imposing height. He had to be at least six-three, almost a foot taller than her own five feet four.

For the briefest of moments, their gazes wed.

His eyes glinted as if he knew exactly what she looked like stark naked and he approved. The intimate suggestion in his stare caused Elle's knees to weaken.

Nature had packaged him in a hard, muscular frame. He was meaty but not bulky. At once both supple and strong. His hands were big and square, his fingernails manicured. Nothing odd there; lots of surgeons babied their hands. Then she spied something that completely rattled her. There, at his wrist, from underneath his Rolex, curled the hint of dark-blue ink.

A tattoo.

Talk about out of place.

Who was he really?

The look that passed between them was succinct and yet weighted with a meaning she couldn't begin to unravel. She felt heavy and light at the same time.

Elle's cheeks tingled. She was blushing!

God, how embarrassing.

What was happening to her? One minute she'd been minding her own business, doing her job as the nursing director of the E.D. and the next minute this sharp-dressed, broad-shouldered stranger had her locked in some emotional chokehold.

She didn't trust a man who could make her feel so breathless with just a look.

Not one little bit.

# 2

As MARK ESCORTED HIM from the emergency department, Dante couldn't help swiveling his head for one last look at the feisty red-haired nurse.

She glowered, hands on her hips, watching him go.

Her eyes narrowed. The woman didn't like him. But could he blame her? He'd messed up her disaster drill, and in the process he could very easily have blown his cover. He'd already made her suspicious.

Not good.

Dante could tell from the way she'd scolded him that she thought he was a bulldozing hothead, and he'd given her plenty of reasons to draw that conclusion. He'd have to be more careful. He threw her the most disarming grin he could conjure before turning his attention back to Mark. Behind him, he heard her snort indignantly. He wasn't winning her over that easily.

"The medical staff is waiting in the doctors' lounge," Mark was saying. "We're throwing you a little welcome party."

Ah crap, he hated this sort of political meet-and-greet, but he knew it was necessary. Suck up to the old guard if you want to fit in, and he had to fit in to gain their trust. He'd done it well enough in college. He could do it again.

"Who's the redhead?" Dante asked, the words popping unexpectedly from his mouth.

"Redhead?"

Dante jerked his thumb in the direction of the emergency department.

Mark wrinkled his nose and his smile disappeared. "Word to the wise, steer clear of Elle."

"Any particular reason?"

"You don't know?"

"Know what?"

"She's my ex-wife."

"For real?"

"We were married for five years."

Surprised, Dante tightened his chin. Elle wasn't Mark's typical type. She was solidly built for one thing—well-rounded hips, sturdy legs, the generous look of a true earth mother. She also had quick, intelligent seashore-blue eyes. Unless his college roommate's tastes had changed, Mark went in for thin, leggy, big-breasted blondes with wide eyes and a minimum of brain power.

Dante resisted the urge to look back down the hallway again. "What happened?"

"Things happen. People change."

"Bad breakup?"

Mark shook his head. "Don't ask."

*She's available.*

It was the wrong thought to think. He should have been wondering what had caused their breakup, but it was too soon to ask probing personal questions of Mark. Tread lightly and trust no one. It was, after all, his lifelong motto.

He had to forget the redhead. The fact that she'd rattled his concentration bothered him almost as much as the rattling itself. He was not a man easily swayed from his objective.

It was the memory of his sister and the filthy alley where her body had been found that had him steeling his mind, clenching his fists. She'd overdosed on heroin, but the medical examiner had found that her death was not accidental. Ligature marks on her wrists had told the tale. She'd been tied up and forcibly injected. She'd been murdered and Dante had never forgiven himself for not protecting her.

As part of his penance, Dante would do whatever it took to bring the bastard responsible for putting Rapture in the underground drug pipeline to justice, and if Mark was that bastard, then so be it.

"Here we are." Mark pushed through the frosted-glass double doors marked *Doctors Only.*

Behind the doors was a collection of well-heeled doctors mingling in an atmosphere of opulence. This room, with its designer draperies, Persian rug, a marble waterfall and chic modern furniture, was a far cry from the sparse, functional doctors' lounge at the county hospital in Dallas where Dante had done his internship.

"Here he is," Mark called out to the gathered contingency. "Our newest plastic surgeon and my old college roommate, Dante Nash."

There was a polite smattering of applause. Someone gave Dante a new scalpel and told him to cut the cake that read in neon-blue buttercream icing, Welcome to Confidential Rejuvenations, Dr. Nash.

He felt like rolling his eyes at the pomp, but in the spirit of cozying up to his new colleagues, he forced a grin. Unsheathing the blade, he then made a precision slice right through the middle of the *N* in his last name.

Someone else handed him a flute of champagne. He felt awkward as hell standing there with a glass of Dom Perignon at nine o'clock in the morning, but he had to act as if he expected such treatment. He forced himself to take a sip.

Mark took him around the room, introducing him to the people gathered.

Dr. Jarrod Butler was the chief of staff. He had a lanky build and a leisurely way of speaking that reminded Dante of Gregory Peck's classic role of Atticus Finch in *To Kill a Mockingbird*. Dante guessed Butler was in his early sixties; he was the most senior person in the room.

The chief of surgery, Wilson Covey, was a few years younger than Butler. He had the square, muscular build of a boxer and wore his salt-and-pepper hair slicked back off his forehead. He had a broad smile and a booming voice that seemed more suited to coaching basketball than practicing medicine.

Together Butler, Covey and Mark co-owned Confidential Rejuvenations. Dante had already met Butler and Covey during his initial interview. Both doctors hailed from a long line of money, and they looked the part. Dignified, impeccably dressed, well-mannered and reserved. They wielded a subtle but undeniable power. What Dante hadn't been able to figure out was how Mark had managed to swing a partnership with these guys.

Beyond those three, there were thirteen other doctors in the lounge, five women, eight men. They held a variety of specialties, particular to a private facility like Confidential Rejuvenations, ranging from psychiatry to substance abuse to antiaging. They were dressed like celebrities in their high-end fashions and designer suits. Clothing targeted at impressing their discerning clientele. The most memorable of the group was a fellow surgeon, a young Latina woman named Vanessa Rodriquez.

Vanessa possessed a firm handshake, cautious eyes and

a penetrating way of looking at him as if she knew exactly who he was and what he was trying to hide. Her stare was unnerving because he could not peg her. Her nails were perfectly manicured, her makeup as flawless as a runway model's. The woman was a beauty with her raven hair and sultry black eyes, but Dante had a thing for redheads. In spite of the care this woman took with her appearance, there was something about the defensive tilt to her shoulders that told him she wasn't entirely comfortable in this group.

Did she have a past she was trying too hard to deny? What was her background? Why was she, at her age, working at a cushy place like Confidential Rejuvenations when she would get so much more experience at a county hospital? The questions intrigued him. He was going to keep a very close eye on Dr. Rodriquez.

She held out a slender hand. He noticed she wasn't having any champagne. "It's nice to have you here, Dr. Nash. And it's encouraging that we're attracting such distinguished talent, especially after what's been happening."

"Excuse me?" Dante raised an eyebrow. "What's been happening?"

She looked surprised. "Mark didn't tell you?"

"About what?" He'd been there less than an hour and already he felt the energy of a dozen hidden secrets.

Vanessa shot a glance at Mark who was deep in conversation with Wilson Covey. "That was unfair of him not to tell you."

"What are you talking about?"

"There've been some…" She paused a moment before finishing with, "unusual occurrences around here lately."

"Unusual occurrences?"

She shrugged and gave him an enigmatic smile.

"Are you always this cryptic?" he asked. "What's the big mystery?"

She ducked her head, lowered her eyes. "I work at Confidential Rejuvenations. As our motto goes, 'You do it, we keep it strictly confidential.'"

"That's the motto?"

Dr. Rodriquez shrugged. "If you have questions, you should talk to Mark. Anyway, welcome aboard. It was nice meeting you, but I've got surgery in thirty minutes." With a wave of her fingertips, she was gone.

Twenty minutes later the welcome reception began breaking up as the doctors wandered off to make morning rounds.

"Come on," Mark inclined his head toward the back exit. "I'll show you to your office."

Dante set down his champagne glass and followed Mark out into the corridor. He was ready to get to work.

They left the hospital proper and took the flagstone path to the physicians' offices at the back of the property. Inside the clean, glossy building Mark introduced him to the perky young receptionist named Hailey. She looked barely out of high school, had a subtle tattoo of a blue butterfly on the inside of her wrist and she blushed when Dante shook her hand.

"Here we are." Mark stopped outside the fifth office on the left and handed Dante a key. He clamped a hand on his shoulder. "I can't tell you how good it is to have you at Confidential Rejuvenations. Feels like old times."

"It's great to be here," Dante said. It wasn't a lie. It was great to be so close to catching the low-life scum who was poisoning people with dangerous designer street drugs.

"I'll let you get settled in," Mark said. "If you need anything, just ask Hailey. I've got rounds, but I'll be back at noon and we can grab some lunch and do a little reminiscing about our football glory days at UT."

He nodded. "Sounds like a plan."

Mark closed the door after him, leaving Dante alone in the office that was three times the size of his office in Quantico. He ran a hand along the polished mahogany desk, spun the leather swivel chair, thickly padded and hand-stitched. His feet sank into the opulent Karastan carpet patterned in a burgundy, black and beige paisley. He walked over to flip the special-order wood blinds covering a wide picture window behind the desk, and his gaze traveled to the built-in floor-to-ceiling bookcases, chock-full of medical tomes, lining two of the four walls.

The place was too cushy, too plush. A doctor could get very soft here. Dante curled his lip in distaste. Was that what had happened to his ex-roommate? Had he gotten so accustomed to living the good life that greed had driven him to start producing Rapture?

*You don't know for sure that Mark is involved. It could be anyone. Covey, Butler, Dr. Rodriquez, the orderly named Ricky, even Elle.*

Dante fisted his hands. He didn't know the answer for sure, but he was going to find out. He remembered Mark's hunger for the finer things in life. They'd both grown up with similar backgrounds—absent mother, abusive father, oldest sibling. And they were both high achievers, striving to escape the dire circumstances they'd been born into. But where Mark placed high values on material possessions and grandiose titles, Dante valued ideals like honor and integrity.

*And revenge.*

It was true. Revenge was a stronger motivator than either honor or integrity. If he wasn't so determined to put Furio Gambezi behind bars for Leeza's death, he wouldn't be undercover, lying about who he was. Spying on people who assumed he was their friend.

The two sides of Dante's personality warred.

The humanitarian part of him was disgusted at how low he'd stooped. But another part of him, the bloodthirsty side, realized the end did indeed justify the means. When Gambezi and the scum who was supplying the gangster with Rapture were off the streets, countless lives would be spared. For that goal, the cost of Dante's integrity was a small price to pay. He couldn't lose sight of it.

Still, he found betraying his own ideals hard to live with. He crossed to the window and opened the blinds, hoping that a glimpse at nature would soothe the battle going on in his head.

Hands jammed into his pockets, he stared out the window to where the verdant field trailed off into a copse of oak and pecan trees. The sky had become overcast since he'd been inside; he remembered the weather report had called for an afternoon drizzle. It had rolled in early from the Colorado River, bringing a gray but compelling dampness.

*Better get to work. You've got to make this look convincing.*

Just as he was about to turn from the window, one of the hospital's side exit doors opened and a woman stepped out.

The flare of auburn hair immediately seized his attention. He took a deep breath. Elle Kingston hesitated on the back porch. Dante noticed she held something clutched in her hands, but he couldn't tell what it was. Furtively she glanced first to the right and then to the left, looking guilty as sin.

Suspicious behavior.

What was she up to?

He narrowed his eyes, watching as she hunched her

shoulders against the drizzle and scurried across the lawn. She paused at the edge of the forest, looked over her shoulder again and then quickly disappeared into the trees.

ELLE SLIPPED INTO the forest, the four cans of almost-expired infant formula that she had boosted from the newborn nursery cradled in her arms. Fear pushed her heart rate higher. Anxiety had her biting her bottom lip.

*Please, please, let the baby be okay,* she prayed.

Worried that she might have been seen, Elle cast one more glance over her shoulder, looking back from where she'd come.

In the foggy drizzle, the five-story hospital built of stylized red stone looked positively gothic with its witch's hat turrets, black slate roof and gingerbread trim. The guarded wrought-iron gates, privacy hedges and trellises twined with English ivy only added to the air of mystery.

Neighbors called it a fortress. Pleased patients dubbed it a sanctuary. *Texas Monthly* had christened Confidential Rejuvenations a place where celebrity secrets go to die.

At times like this, with gray weather enshrouding those stony walls, the place made Elle feel exquisitely sad at the thought of all those people with so much to hide.

The thing of it was, in spite of her occasionally mixed feelings about Confidential Rejuvenations and the work they did here, she loved her job. And she was concerned over the strange goings-on of the recent weeks. First there'd been the media leaks, then the arson in the laundry room. After that, several items had gone missing. Strange things like a ham from the kitchen, crutches from central supply, a crate of bleach from the janitor's closet.

Taken one by one, the occurrences were nothing more than criminal mischief, but added together, it didn't seem like a coincidence. Elle was beginning to wonder if someone was purposely trying to sabotage the hospital. The idea that someone was intentionally doing harm to the place she loved angered her.

She shook off her fanciful thoughts. There was no time for this. She had to make this quick. She had less than an hour left on her lunch break.

Resolutely she pushed deeper into the woods. After several minutes of hiking, she passed the meditation sanctuary tucked away in a grotto of trees. The overgrowth of vines crawling across the walkway leading to the structure told her no groundskeepers had been up here to maintain it in a very long time. Patients seeking solitude rarely visited this sanctuary since they'd built a bigger one down by the river. More often it was used illicitly for romantic trysts by patients and hospital staff alike. Elle narrowed her eyes as she walked past, wondering if anyone was inside. But the windows were tinted, keeping passersby from peeking in.

The grounds of Confidential Rejuvenations encompassed over a hundred acres, most of it covered by the thick grove of indigenous trees that ran parallel to the river. Walking paths extended throughout the forest in several directions, but Elle diverged from the beaten trail.

Instead, she ducked under the branch of an aged oak and stepped over a moss-covered fallen log, keeping her eyes to the ground. Several minutes later, she saw what she was searching for—faint footprints in the mud.

Yes. It had to be near.

She crouched, studying the undergrowth, looking for any signs of the baby. Growing up with brothers and a father who hunted, Elle had learned through osmosis a tracking trick or two. She set down the bottles of formula and moved deeper into the undergrowth.

"Where are you little guy?" Elle cooed and pushed aside the thick carpeting of monkey grass slicked with fine beads of rain. "Come out, come out wherever you are. I might not be mama, but I've got food."

Then she heard a twig crack loudly on the path she'd abandoned.

Startled, she rocked back on her heels, hand to her throat, pulse pounding, and jerked her head around. Peering through the newly budded leaves, she stared at the broad-shouldered man silhouetted in the tunnel of trees.

She recognized him immediately as he stood there looking very out of his element in his tailored silk suit. His intense, dark eyes drilled into her as if he could see deep down inside to all the things she tried so hard to hide— her fears, her insecurities, her doubts, the dark secrets she told no one, not even her best friends.

The little hop of sexual excitement catching low in her belly took Elle by surprise.

"Looking for something?" asked Dr. Dante Nash, his voice as cool as well water.

His presence threw her off balance and Elle hated being in a defensive position. She rose to her feet.

"You followed me," she accused.

"I did," he admitted without the slightest hint of apology in his voice.

"Why?"

Tree branches separated them. Dante on the path. Elle ankle-deep in the undergrowth, studying him like a cautious child peering from around her mother's skirt. He made her feel things she didn't want to feel—interest, attraction, compulsion and possibility.

He shrugged. "Curiosity."

She narrowed her eyes. "Are you spying on me?"

His smile was slight and didn't reach his light brown eyes. She found herself wondering when was the last time the man had genuinely smiled, and then Elle wondered why she was wondering.

"Why?" he asked. "Are you up to something that would invite spying?"

Oh, he was good, answering a question with a question, turning things around on her. His cagey manner made her bristle. Mark had been equally adept at evading her questions.

"No," she denied, realizing just how defensive she sounded.

He glanced at the baby bottles she'd settled on the ground at her feet. "What's that all about?"

She stepped in front of the baby bottles, blocking his view. Her gaze tracked over him, over the fine lines of his suit, growing damper every minute he stood in the drizzle. She was getting wet as well. She could feel her unruly hair growing frizzier by the second. "I really don't think it's any of your concern."

"I don't know about that," Dante said. "Looks to me as if that baby formula came from the supply closet of Confidential Rejuvenations."

"What if it did?"

"That's theft in anyone's book. Are you a thief, Elle Kingston?" His eyes locked with hers and he never looked away.

It was damned disconcerting. A buzz of sexual energy sizzled down her neck.

"What are you?" she snapped. "A cop?"

For a moment so brief she was sure she must have imagined it, a look of uneasiness passed over his face. He moved closer, pushing the soggy tree branches out of his way, and with each step toward her, Elle's heart beat harder and her breath grew more shallow. He stopped within an arm's length of her and she quelled the sudden urge to reach out to run her fingers over his strong, commanding jaw and fit the tip of her finger into the cleft at his chin.

"Mark's been talking to me about buying into Confidential Rejuvenations," he said. "It's in my best interest to know if the hospital has a big problem with employee theft."

"The formula expires in two days. It would be thrown out anyway." She didn't owe this man an explanation, so why was she giving him one?

"Who's the formula for?"

Good grief, why wouldn't he just go away and leave her in peace?

But he just kept staring at her, one eyebrow quirked up on his forehead, that irritating half smile hanging on the corner of his too-tempting mouth.

She glared. "Don't you have patients to see?"

"Nope. It's my first day. No patients yet."

"Then go unpack your stethoscope or something."

"Already unpacked."

She glowered at him.

He shrugged. She could tell he was enjoying jerking her chain. "I was bored," he said. "Following you seemed like more fun than staring at the four walls of my office."

"And I'm busy."

He glanced around at the forest. "Doing what?"

"That's none of your business, Dr. Nash," she replied tartly.

"What are you hiding, Nurse Kingston?"

The seductive way he said her name sent flames of lust licking through her belly. This was ridiculous, the way her traitorous body was reacting.

"Nothing," she denied.

"No?"

She shook her head.

"Then why are you outside in the rain, while your hair goes wild all over your head?"

"I'm a water nymph in disguise," she retorted.

His smile broadened and for the first time it reached his eyes. A real smile. "I can see that," he murmured. "So much fiery red hair."

He closed the short distance between them until the toes of his sleek black Gucci shoes, dotted with water sprinkles, were almost butted up against her white leather nurse's clogs. The dark flicker in his eyes sent alarm bells ringing inside her as he reached up to finger a strand of her frizzed-out locks.

She gulped, unable to find her voice, not knowing what she would say even if she found it. He was the most enigmatic man she'd ever met, and he made her feel that if she were to peel back the complicated layers of his personality, she could dig endlessly and never find his true center. How did a woman ever learn to trust a man she couldn't know?

*I dunno, how come you trusted Mark?*

Because she dumbly loved too easily, loved too hard. But no more. She was done with opening her heart too fully, too soon. She was finished with blind loyalty. From now on, she was going to be cautious and cynical and distrustful.

Dante's fingers lingered at her hair. "No secrets at all, water nymph? Nothing you want to get off your chest? Nothing to confess?"

She could scarcely think. The heat from his body, the fragrance of his captivatingly masculine cologne mixed with the musky scent of damp forest rattled her brain.

"Nothing."

"I don't believe you," he said, his hot, laser-sharp gaze

puncturing hers. "A smart woman like you, who knows how to keep other people's secrets, is bound to have a few secrets of her own."

Her nipples tightened to hard buds underneath her scrub top. She was glad for her lab coat buttoned up over her clothes. Still, in this rain…

She stifled the urge to look down and see if her arousal was visible through her scrubs. But she didn't want to turn his attention in that direction, so she simply tried her best to look cool and calm.

"Spoken like a man who's dying to reveal a few skeletons from *his* closet," she countered.

He took his fingers from her hair, but he did not lower his hand. Rather, he stroked the back of one finger along the line of her jaw.

His touch was like fire. She swallowed, forced herself not to shudder.

"A fringe of raindrops," he explained. "On your chin."

Elle sucked in her breath, stepped back away from him, away from his exploring fingers that sent heated lightning shooting straight to her womb. He was looking at her with the most compelling expression on his face. She watched his eyes drift to the tell-tale throbbing of her pulse at the juncture of her throat and collarbone.

*What was with this guy?*

A soft noise from the undergrowth drew their attention to the ground.

That's when Elle saw what she'd come into the forest searching for—a fawn with wide, terrified eyes.

Her nurturing instincts vanquished any weak-kneed fantasies she might be having about the man beside her. Heedless of the mud, she knelt on the carpet of pine needles and dead leaves and reached out to the baby.

The fawn trembled at her touch, unable to run, even to stand on its wobbly little legs.

"That's your secret?" Dante sounded strangely relieved.

All business now, Elle looked up at him. This baby needed her. She had no time for sexy thoughts. "Hand me one of those bottles, will you?"

Dante leaned over to retrieve the bottle as Elle gathered the fawn into her arms and tucked it in the crook of her left elbow. He straightened and turned to hand her the formula. His forearm brushed lightly against her shoulder. She caught a closer glimpse of the steely set of his jaw where the hint of a five o'clock shadow had started to sprout. A whiff of his woodsy cologne set her heart pumping. Oh boy, this wasn't good. Not good at all.

*Forget about him.*

Resolutely, she focused her attention on the fawn squirming in her arms. Gently she placed the bottle's nipple on the baby's lower lip. She bent it slightly to express a squirt of milk.

The fawn tentatively flicked out its tongue. Once it tasted the milk, the baby made greedy sucking noises and it was easy for Elle to slip the nipple into its hungry little mouth.

"How did you know the fawn was here?" Dante asked, crouching beside her, his deep voice as comforting as hot chocolate on a cold winter day.

"I've been watching a pregnant doe from the back window of the E.D.," she said. "Every morning she crosses over from the farms to the road and heads down to the river. Two days ago, she didn't cross. Then yesterday, when she went down to the water, I noticed she wasn't pregnant any longer. Then this morning…" She let her words trail off and took a deep breath to keep the tears from her voice. "After the disaster drill, we had a motor vehicle collision victim come into the E.D. for stitches. The driver hit a doe in the road and rolled his SUV. I just knew…"

Elle pressed her lips together. A tear slid down her cheek. Ah dammit, she was crying. Why was she crying? She was an E.D. nurse. She'd seen a lot worse things than a dead deer. She blinked and sniffled back the tears.

Dante clamped a hand on her forearm and squeezed gently. "It's okay to feel tender-hearted over an orphaned baby."

Just like that, he got her.

Mark would have told her she was being ridiculous. Mark, the same man who'd kept promising her they'd start a family next year, then the next and the next, until finally he left her for a much younger woman who clearly did not have a ticking biological clock.

The fawn wriggled in her arms. It made a soft bleating noise of complaint. What was she doing wrong? The baby chewed the nipple. Milk squirted every which way. Elle was having trouble holding the animal—the rambunctious youngster was stronger than it looked. The fawn kicked at her with its rowdy little hooves, butted the bottle with its head. The formula flew from her hands and landed in the bushes.

"Oh fiddlecakes," she said, and reached for a second bottle.

"Fiddlecakes?" He sounded amused. "I thought the term was *fiddlesticks*."

"Something my grandmother used to say. I spent a lot of time with her growing up. Both my parents did shift work."

"Medical?"

"Cops."

An odd expression she couldn't read crossed Dante's

face. Then he surprised her by plunking down beside her on the ground. "Give him here."

"What are you doing?"

"Let me hold him and you can hold the bottle."

"You're going to get mud on your suit."

"I don't care."

"Really?" That surprised her. Mark would rather have his teeth pulled than sit on the ground in one of his tailored suits.

"It's just clothing."

That didn't sound like any surgeon she knew. This guy was a horse of a different color. Elle cocked her head to study him. "Why are you getting involved?"

"Just give him to me," Dante said, clearly not someone who liked explaining himself.

"How do you know it's a him?"

"I had a good view of his backside while you had him tucked under your arm." Dante took the fawn from her and held him in his lap with a firm grip.

His hand grazed hers.

The breath knotted tight in Elle's chest, unable to find a way out. Hand tingling, she ducked her head and got up to retrieve the second bottle.

Together they sat side by side on the muddy forest floor, raindrops dotting their skin as they nourished an orphaned baby buck.

Her estimation of Dante Nash shot up a notch. She could tell he was a good doctor by the considerate way he held the deer. Gentle but firm. It was the kind of touch that would make any patient feel safe in his hands. She slanted a sideways glance at his face and discovered he was looking at her.

Their eyes met.

He winked.

A hot flush of sexual excitement raced through her. To Elle there was nothing sexier than a nurturing man. Quickly she dropped her gaze. No, no, she didn't want this feeling. She did not want to like him. To *want* him. She'd just come out of a miserable divorce. This wasn't the time for a relationship, and he, as one of her ex-husband's friends, was not someone she should choose.

"You're going to have to take him to the animal rescue center," Dante said.

"I know." Elle stroked the baby's fur.

"Yet you're getting attached anyway."

She shrugged. "A fault of mine. Getting attached when I shouldn't."

"It's not a fault. Just means you care."

"Yeah well, it makes for a frequently broken heart."

A long silence stretched between them, interrupted only by the sounds of the baby deer suckling. He finished one bottle and Elle started the famished youngster on another.

"Why'd you marry Mark?" he asked.

"What?" His question caught her off guard. She raised her head, stared at him again. "What do you mean?"

"Don't get offended," Dante said. "It's just that you're not Mark's usual type."

"No?" Of course not, Elle thought. Cassandra was Mark's usual type—blond, beautiful and busty. Elle stared down at her own average-sized 34B bosom.

"You're too smart for him."

"You don't even know me. How can you say that?"

"You have lively eyes."

Elle snorted, but his words brought a heated rush of pleasure to her cheeks.

"Let me guess, you put Mark through medical school.

Worked a full-time job, paid the bills and helped him with his homework."

Dante was so right it hurt. "You know what?" Elle said. "That's none of your business."

"Touché," Dante said. "He's through."

"Who? Mark?"

"No, the fawn."

Indeed, the baby had sucked the bottle dry. Feeling an odd strangeness she couldn't quite identify, Elle got to her feet and swiped at the mud on the knees of her scrubs. "My lunch hour is over. They'll be wondering where I am."

Dante stood up, the fawn cradled in his arms. "What are we going to do with him?"

Elle reached out for the baby. "I'll call my sister-in-law. She's interning for the vet at the end of the road. She'll know who to call about disposing of the fawn's mother and what to do about this little guy."

Dante transferred the deer to her arms, their fingers brushing again in the process. Suddenly her heart was in her throat and she had no excuse for it.

"So tell me," she said. "Did you satisfy your curiosity? Or are you still bored?"

He lowered his eyelids and gave her a sultry look. He raked his gaze over the length of her body, then went back to stare at her lips. He looked like a man whose appetite had just been whetted.

Then he said in low, provocative voice, "Not by a long shot."

The baby kicked and she almost dropped him. Elle tightened her grip on the fawn and told her silly heart to stop beating so fast. The look Dante was giving her meant absolutely nothing.

# 3

HALF AN HOUR LATER, the animal control people came to haul away the mother deer's carcass, while Elle's sister-in-law, Charlotte, arrived in a van to pick up the fawn.

Elle stood at the back entrance to the hospital cradling the trembling animal in her arms, Dante at her side. She wondered why he was sticking around, but she didn't ask.

"Ooh, Elle," said her sister-in-law's assistant, Linda when she spied the baby. Linda was a middle-aged woman with a welcoming smile, dimples in both cheeks and dog hair all over her lab jacket. "Look what you've got there."

The receptionist looked from the fawn to Elle and then to Dante, and then an appreciative gleam came into her eyes. The look on Linda's face proved Elle's suspicion that the man attracted feminine attention wherever he went.

Charlotte came around to the front of the van where Elle, Dante and Linda were standing. Elle's sister-in-law wore her dark-brown hair in a short, stylish cut that accentuated her gamine features. Underneath her lab jacket she wore jeans, a yellow T-shirt and scuffed cowboy boots. She was wiry and petite. Elle had a hard time imagining her wrangling large farm animals.

Charlotte immediately zeroed in on the fawn. "What happened?"

"His mom got hit by a car. Animal control came for her."

Charlotte sighed. "Poor little guy." She turned to Dante. "Hi." She stuck out a hand. "My name's Charlotte. I'm married to Elle's younger brother, Tom."

"Dante Nash," he said and shook Charlotte's hand. "Nice to meet you."

"Dante's the new surgeon at Confidential Rejuvenations," Elle explained. "He was with me when I found the fawn."

"Oh really?" Charlotte got that matchmaking look in her eyes. Ever since she'd married Tom, Charlotte was relentless about trying to hook up her single friends and family members. She was still in the starry-eyed honeymoon phase, convinced that marriage was the solution to everyone's problems. "So tell me, are you married, Dr. Nash?"

"I'm not."

"No?" Charlotte glanced at Elle and wriggled her eyebrows suggestively.

"Dante was Mark's best friend in college," Elle said and sent Charlotte a look that said forget about fixing me up.

"Not best friends," Dante corrected. "Mark and I were just roommates and football teammates."

"There you go," Charlotte said. "Clearly he knows Mark's true colors if he's not claiming him as a friend. Score one for Dante."

"Char," Elle said through gritted teeth. "This fawn is getting heavy."

"Oh yeah, sorry. Right this way." She led them to the back of the van where she opened up the double doors, and Elle settled the fawn down on the floor.

Dante stood behind Elle, silently watching the proceedings. Elle felt weird having him hang out with her, especially after what Charlotte had just said, and she wondered what on earth he must be thinking.

"I gave him some baby formula from the hospital nursery," Elle said.

Charlotte looked up, a serious expression on her face, the matchmaking temporarily forgotten. "Good thing you found him when you did. If he'd been out in the cold overnight without his mom, I hate to think what would have happened. Either coyotes or bobcats would probably have gotten him. You saved his life, Elle."

Warmth spread from the center of her heart outward in a sweet glow. Elle smiled and softly scratched the fawn behind one ear. She'd saved a life. Nothing made her feel happier than that.

"I'll keep him at the office for a while, make sure he's going to be okay and then we'll take him to Dr. Levy's sanctuary." Dr. Levy was the vet Charlotte was training under and he had donated several hundred acres along the Colorado River as an animal sanctuary.

"Thanks. I knew you'd know what to do."

Charlotte looked over at her assistant. "Hop in the back with the baby, Linda. I'll drive."

"Will do."

Linda climbed inside the back of the van. Elle gave the little buck one last parting look and sighed wistfully as Charlotte shut the door.

"Elle's going to make a great mother someday," Charlotte said to Dante. "She's so good with babies, whatever the species."

"No doubt," Dante said.

Elle sneaked a glance over at him, but she couldn't read a thing from his impassive face.

*Sorry for my matchmaking sister-in-law,* she telegraphed him with her eyes.

He gave her an enigmatic smile and a slight shrug as if to say: *Family, what are you going to do?*

"Are you still planning on coming to the family softball tournament? It's three weeks from Saturday," Charlotte asked Elle. "Tom's ordering this year's jerseys and I need a head count."

"As if I could skip out. Dad would never let me hear the end of it if I didn't show." Elle said. The first weekend in May the Kingstons staged an annual family reunion centered around a weekend-long softball tournament. It had been a family tradition long before Elle was born.

Charlotte tucked her fingers into the back pockets of her jeans and sized up Dante. "Why don't you come, too?" she asked. "Our team is short a catcher since Mark divorced Elle. If you don't come we'll be forced to play Aunt Gertie."

Mortified at her sister-in-law's forwardness, Elle couldn't bring herself to look at Dante. "Char, for heaven's sake, let it be. Dante has no interest in playing softball with the Kingston clan."

"Maybe not," Char said. "But he might have interest in spending some time with you."

*Kill me now,* Elle thought.

"Thank you for the invitation," Dante said. "It sounds like a lot of fun, but I have to check and see if I'm scheduled to be on call that weekend."

"Just know that we'd love to have you," Charlotte said. "Aunt Gertie can't catch to save her life."

"We've gotta go now. Thanks for looking after the deer." Elle said, and then lowered her voice so only Charlotte could hear her. "You are *so* dead."

Her sister-in-law laughed. "You'll thank me on your golden anniversary."

"I gotta get back to work," Elle said, turned on her heel and hurried back inside the hospital before her matchmaking sister-in-law found yet another way to embarrass her.

AFTER ELLE WENT BACK inside the hospital, Dante returned to the office to find Mark waiting for him.

Mark took one look at the damp, muddy suit that would have cost Dante half a month's salary if he'd been the one to pay for it and shook his head. "Hell, man, what happened to you?"

"Got lost in the forest."

"Huh? What were you doing in the woods?"

"Never mind." Dante shook his head. "Where could I get a set of scrubs to change into?"

Mark shook his head. "No, no, we're going to lunch in Austin with Covey and Butler. You can't wear scrubs." Mark eyed the width of Dante's shoulders. "We're still about the same size. You can wear one of my suits."

"You keep extra suits at the office?"

"Don't you?"

"You forget," Dante said, following Mark into his office. "I've been working for a county hospital."

That was the phony cover the FBI had provided for his résumé. And he'd worked at enough county hospitals as both an intern and resident that he knew they were as different from Confidential Rejuvenations as Park Avenue was from the streets of Baghdad.

Mark stepped to a mahogany wardrobe in the corner of his massive office and threw open the door. Inside were four suits, all much more expensive than the one Dante was wearing. "Long way from our UT dorm days, huh?"

"You've done very well, Mark." Dante selected a navy-blue suit from the wardrobe and looked over at his colleague. They'd shared a dorm room and the football field, but they hadn't been the best of friends, mainly because Dante never let anyone get that close. Still, he couldn't help feeling like something of a traitor.

*If Mark's involved in this mess, he's going down. You have no reason to feel guilty.*

No, he shouldn't feel guilty, but lying didn't come easily. "Thanks for the loaner," he said. "I'll go change."

After returning to his office, Dante closed the blinds on his window before changing into the clean suit. As he reached for the string on the louvered blinds, he found his gaze drifting to the edge of the forest and his memory flashed back to Elle.

He thought about how she'd looked with her auburn hair curling up around her face in the rain. She really could have been a water nymph with her dewy skin, mischievous lips and womanly figure.

The setting hadn't been sexual, but he'd gotten aroused. It had taken every bit of the self-control he possessed not to kiss her. When Dante had touched her hair, he'd come so damned close to falling into the abyss.

It scared him.

Not only because she was just as much a suspect as anyone else at Confidential Rejuvenations, but because she made him feel things he had no business feeling.

He wanted to take her to bed.

Bed? Hell, he'd wanted to take her right there on the forest floor.

And she'd looked at him as if she wouldn't resist.

Then he thought about how tender she'd been with the baby deer. A true earth mother. That thought made him feel something else entirely. Longing, sadness and a bitter-sweet loneliness he hadn't experienced since his mother had taken off when he was a kid.

He smiled, remembering about how flustered she'd gotten over her sister-in-law's matchmaking attempts. Clearly Elle was still touchy on the subject of marriage, not that he could blame her. From all accounts, she'd been through a rough time with the divorce.

Dante shook off thoughts of Elle along with his muddy suit. He was a professional, an undercover FBI agent. These emotions could only trip him up. There were only two feelings he could afford to indulge in.

One was justice.

The other was revenge.

Elle Kingston was Mark's Achilles' heel. No one knew more about a man than his wife. And no one could flip faster than an ex-wife scorned. She was Dante's route to Lawson's downfall.

He knew then what he had to do. He must capitalize on the chemistry between them. Get closer to her. Find out exactly what secrets she was keeping about her ex-husband. He would have to use her, manipulate her and then, in the end, he was going to have to walk away.

It was a dirty job.

But he'd been assigned to do it and Dante Nash never shirked his duty.

TWO DAYS AFTER ELLE'S strange encounter in the woods with Dante, she met her two best friends, Vanessa and Julie, at Stevie B's, a popular blues bar down by the marina, not far from Confidential Rejuvenations. They met once a week, usually on hump day, to blow off steam and offer each other moral support. It was a weekly ritual

Elle had come to rely on since her divorce. She had no idea how she would have made it through such a rough patch if it hadn't been for her friends.

Elle was the last one to arrive. Vanessa and Julie were already sitting at a casual picnic style table in the back overlooking the Colorado River. Catamarans glided majestically through the water, the setting sun cast golden lights over the sails. It was early, the crowd was still light. The band wouldn't start playing for another hour.

Vanessa and Julie weren't watching the boats. Instead, they were engrossed in a game of "Sex or Dinner" and they hadn't seen her come in.

"Jerry Seinfeld," Julie said to Vanessa with a toss of her ash-blond hair.

Julie was one of those petite women who men seemed to instantly gravitate toward and want to take care of. Even dressed in the pink scrubs of the newborn nursery where she worked as a registered nurse, Julie looked incredibly feminine. She had a certain romantic naiveté about her that didn't jive with the earthy, no-nonsense personality shared by the majority of nurses. If Julie weren't so darned sweet, Elle would have been jealous of her.

"Strictly dinner," Vanessa answered. "Jerry's funny, but sexy he's not. How about Colin Ferrell."

"Seriously, you have to ask?" Julie blushed.

"I gotcha, chica." Vanessa flashed a sly smile. "Sex all the way with that delicious Irishman."

"Sex sounds fabulous," Julie said, "but you know I'd be too shy to see it through. Good thing Colin is just the stuff of my midnight fantasies."

"What about that cowboy sitting over there on the bar stool underneath the Coors sign?" Vanessa nodded at a lean-muscled, good-looking man in a Stetson at the end of the bar. "Sex or dinner?"

"Hmm," Julie said. "This game makes me nervous when it leaves the realm of celebrity fantasies."

"Please, you've been working at Confidential Rejuvenations long enough to know that celebrities are no different than the rest of us. They just think they are. I mean come on, Mark managed to snag Cassandra Roberts."

"But Mark is rich and good-looking and a doctor."

"So sex or dinner with Mark?"

Julie shuddered. "Neither. Besides the fact he's Elle's ex, there's something about him that's just…"

"Hi, guys," Elle said, rushing to let her friends know she was standing there before they kept talking about Mark. She plunked down beside Julie and hooked her purse over the back of her chair. "I had to restock the crash cart before I left work. We had a code at the end of the shift. A teenager."

"Oh gosh, it's especially awful when it's a kid. Survivor?" Julie asked, nibbling her bottom lip.

Elle nodded and smiled triumphantly. It was always a good day when they saved a life. "We got her back."

"That's great news," Vanessa said.

Because of patient confidentiality, Elle couldn't discuss the case with her friends, although she longed to tell them what had happened and get their opinion on the odd turn of events. The daughter of a high-ranking local political official had collapsed at her private high school. The school had called an ambulance and they'd rushed her to the E.D., but by the time she rolled through the doors, she wasn't breathing. A few seconds later, the girl had gone into full-blown cardiac arrest and they had to call a code.

One of the girl's friends, who'd been escorted to the hospital by the police, had confessed that she'd taken a pill they'd bought the weekend before from some guy they'd met at a rave. The lab had drawn blood samples from the victim, but they'd been unable to detect any drugs in her system, so they'd sent the samples out for more rigorous testing at a specialized lab.

According to the victim's friend, the pill was supposed to make you feel sexy and floaty and in love with everyone. It was a lot like Ecstasy, she'd said, only sexier.

"We ordered a pitcher of raspberry beer and chicken nachos for appetizers," Vanessa said.

"Sounds great." Elle slipped out of her cardigan. "Because of the code, I missed lunch. I'm starving."

"So," Vanessa asked her. "How's your week been so far?"

Elle started to tell them about Dante, but what was there to tell? She was attracted to another man for the first time since her divorce. Big deal. It couldn't go anywhere. "Nothing unusual."

"That's not what I heard." Julie reached for the pitcher the waitress set on the table along with three frosted mugs and began pouring up the beer. She tilted the glass to keep too much foam from forming.

"What did you hear?" Vanessa leaned forward.

"I heard Elle went into the woods alone on Monday and she came out with a baby and a man." Julie grinned impishly and slid a mug of beer in front of Elle.

"What?" Vanessa jerked her gaze from Julie to Elle, her dark Latina eyes flashing with interest.

"It was a baby deer." Quickly, Elle explained how she'd come to find the fawn.

"What did you do with it?"

"Charlotte came and got it," she said. "The vet she works for has an animal sanctuary. They say the fawn's going to be fine."

"Except that he's an orphan," Vanessa said gloomily. She'd had a difficult childhood and had the tendency to look on the dark side of life.

Elle studied her two friends who were so different, not only in looks but temperament, as well. Julie was the timid, tenderhearted romantic who saw the world through rose-colored glasses. Vanessa was the bold, sharp-witted cynic with a fiery temper.

And her?

Well, Elle was the center. Neither sweet nor tart. Neither too timid nor too daring. Tepid. Average. Nothing special. Elle supposed that was one reason they were all such good friends. They balanced each other out.

"So what about the guy?" Vanessa asked.

"What guy?" Elle evaded, even though she wasn't really sure why she didn't want to talk about Dante. Usually, she told Julie and Vanessa everything.

"The guy from the forest." Vanessa took a sip of her beer and eyed Elle over the rim of her mug with an assessing stare.

"There was no 'guy' from the forest," Elle said lightly. "It was just that new doctor, Dante Nash. He saw me go into the forest and thought maybe something was wrong and I needed help. He has a bit of a rescuer complex."

"What do you mean by that?" Julie asked, and dove into the platter of chicken nachos the waitress deposited in the middle of the table along with three plates.

Elle told them what had happened in the E.D. on the day Dante arrived and busted up her disaster drill.

"Hmm." Julie grinned. "I think something more might be afoot here."

"What do you mean?"

"What if Dr. Nash is really into you?"

"I don't care if he's into me or not. I'm not into him."
*Keep lying like that and your nose is going to grow.*

"I met him," Vanessa said. "He's very sexy, if a bit aloof. Why don't you let him rescue you?" She winked boldly. "If you get my drift."

"For one thing, I don't need rescuing. Julie's the one who's into rescue fantasies," she said.

Julie held up her palms. "Hey, after what happened with Roger, I'm through with love. At least for the foreseeable future. For now, all I want is hot sex."

"I don't want love or hot sex." Elle nibbled at a nacho. "I just need a nice guy to be nice to me."

"No, no." Julie shook her head. "You can't settle for less than you deserve. You deserve fireworks, great sex and a nice guy. Problem is, I fear such a man is a mythological creature."

"Julie's on the right track, Elle," Vanessa said. "You need a wild fling to cleanse your palate after Mark before you jump headlong into a new relationship and motherhood. You definitely need a rebound guy."

"Julie's twenty-five—she doesn't have a biological clock that keeps going off every two minutes. She can afford to have meaningless flings. I'm thirty-two and not getting any younger. I'm past the point of caring about chemistry. Mark and I had chemistry. At least in the beginning we did, and look how that ended up. Besides, another thing against Dante is that he's Mark's college roommate, and from the stories Mark tells, the guy was a real player."

"Playboys are perfect for meaningless affairs," Vanessa said. "That way nobody gets hurt."

"Maybe he's not a playboy anymore. People can change," Julie pointed out. "I'm trying to change. I'm not as shy as I used to be and I did work up the courage to give Roger the boot."

"You're looking at this the wrong way," Vanessa argued. "You need a rebound guy that wants to give you nothing but sex. Someone gorgeous and totally inappropriate for you. That way you can get past the hurt Mark caused."

"I'm not following you."

"Stick it to Mark the way he stuck it to you. Think how jealous he'll be when he finds out you're sleeping with his college roommate." Vanessa tapped a perfectly manicured nail against the Formica tabletop.

"That's petty," Elle said, but she had to admit the thought held some appeal. She wasn't proud of her less-than-noble instincts, but she was human. It would eat at Mark's craw if she had fling with his old friend. The way he'd treated her, he deserved it.

And there was the delicious fact that she found Dante extremely attractive. It wasn't too difficult picturing the two of them in bed. Their legs intertwined, sheets tousled, bodies slick with the sheen of lovemaking. Especially since it had been a long time since she'd enjoyed that kind of intimacy.

"Payback's a bitch." Vanessa grinned.

"I couldn't."

"Why not?"

"What if he's not interested?"

"He went into the forest after you, didn't he?"

Vanessa had a point. She was pretty sure Dante was attracted to her. "I wouldn't know how to start."

"Just seduce him."

"You make it sound as if it's as easy as making a peanut butter sandwich."

"For her," Julie said, "it probably is. Nessa, you gotta remember, Elle and I don't have the same powers of seduction that you do."

Vanessa snorted. "Of course you do. You seriously underestimate yourselves. Both of you. Men are so easy. Feed them, don't talk to them during sporting events and go down on them every now and then and they're happy."

Elle thought of the dark look in Dante's eyes. She hugged herself and shivered against the memory that sent a fresh tingle of sensation tripping up her spine. "I have the feeling Dr. Nash is a lot more complicated than most men."

"He does seem rather enigmatic, but that makes the challenge all the more exciting, don't you think?" Vanessa rubbed her palms together gleefully.

In theory, a strictly sexual affair sounded good, but in reality, Elle knew it wasn't that simple. Sex changed things and she'd never been one of those women who could take pleasure in a physical encounter that held no emotional component. That belief hadn't protected her, however. She'd given her heart to Mark, tried her best to make their marriage work and she'd ended up hurting more than she'd ever known it was possible to hurt.

For the past fourteen months she'd been floundering, not knowing what her identity was now that she was no longer anyone's wife. She and Mark had moved in together when she was right out of nursing school. She'd only had a couple of lovers before him and none since.

*So maybe Vanessa was right. Maybe it was time for a change. Maybe it was time to try on a new identity.*

A part of her was so scared. Terrified to take a risk. She had to do something to ease the emptiness she felt inside. But the very idea of a carefree fling made her palms sweat and brought a sick feeling to the pit of her stomach.

No, she simply couldn't have a casual affair. Not yet. Not now.

And most certainly not with Dante Nash.

# 4

FOR THE NEXT TWO WEEKS, every morning at eight o'clock Elle took her fifteen-minute coffee break in the E.D. employee lounge just so she could peer out the rear window and watch Dante's magnificent Porsche Carrera GT pull into the doctors' parking lot. The only thing that spoiled her new ritual was that Mark's Ferrari pulled up at the same time.

Holding the blinds open with two fingers, she peered out, sipping her soy latte, purposefully ignoring Mark, while her gaze lingered on Dante's well-shaped backside as he walked up the flagstone pathway to his office.

He was gorgeous. Tall and impressively muscular but not overdeveloped. His dark hair brushed back off his forehead. His chiseled shoulders showcased so splendidly in his expensive business suit. She wished for a pair of binoculars.

She heard the whoop of the ambulance pulling into the bay outside, but her mind barely registered the noise. They were expecting a feverish elderly woman from the upscale Alzheimer's treatment facility down the road—not exactly an emergency. Her highly competent staff could handle the transfer while she indulged in a few seconds more of ogling Dr. Nash's backside.

But this morning Dante suddenly stopped in the middle of the sidewalk and slowly turned his head.

Elle gulped.

His eyes met hers. The look was so intense she gasped, dropped the blinds, took a step back and stumbled against the break room table so hard it shook.

Ouch. That was going to leave a bruise.

"Gracious, Elle, are you okay?"

Elle looked up to see Maxine Woodbury standing in the doorway, juggling a cup of cinnamon-scented tea and a bagel with cream cheese.

"Fine." Elle forced a smile.

Maxine settled her breakfast on the table, and then went to peer out the blinds. The woman was a phenomenal secretary, and she was as nosy as a bloodhound. Her heightened curiosity was probably the reason she still worked at Confidential Rejuvenations at sixty-eight. Working here, Maxine was privy to as many secrets as if she worked at the *National Enquirer.* Good thing she also knew how to keep her mouth shut.

Maxine clucked her tongue and turned back to her breakfast. "You've got to stop pining over that man."

"What?" For a moment, Elle feared the astute ward secretary had somehow learned about this silly infatuation she'd developed for Dante. She pretended to tighten the bell on the stethoscope dangling around her neck so Maxine couldn't get a good look at her flushed cheeks.

"He did you dirty. You've got to let him go. Forget him. Find someone new," she advised.

"Oh, you mean Mark."

Maxine's eyes perked up with interest. "Who else would you be staring at out that window that made you look so unsettled?"

"I'm not unsettled," Elle denied, and absentmindedly rubbed the side of her hip where she'd whacked it on the table.

"No?" Maxine got up and headed for the window.

Elle snapped the blinds closed and turned to Maxine, hands behind her back. "My staring out the window has nothing to do with anything."

"Uh-hmm." Maxine said with a wink as if she didn't believe it for a minute.

"It doesn't."

"Are his initials *D.N.?*" Maxine smiled knowingly.

Before Elle had a chance to respond, the public address system crackled. "Code Blue, E.D. room three. Code Blue, E.D. room three."

Instinct catapulted Elle from the lounge. A burst of adrenaline shot her into exam room three. She figured the code was on the feverish Alzheimer's patient who must have taken a turn for the worse.

But when she bolted through the door on the heels of a respiratory therapist, Elle was dismayed to see that the lifeless body on the stretcher belonged not to a fragile senior citizen but to a teenage boy.

Her nurses were in full code mode. Jenny Lucas was giving the teenager chest compressions. Heather Newcom was starting an IV with a large-bore needle. One of the paramedics who'd brought the victim in was pumping oxygen into him with an Ambu bag. The other paramedic was rapidly writing everything down on the young man's medical chart.

"Name?" Elle barked at the scribbling paramedic.

"Travis Russell. He's Pete Russell's kid."

Pete Russell was a well-known Austin musician who'd made it big fusing country and western lyrics with a hip-hop beat.

Elle assessed the boy's condition. His skin was dusky, his body flaccid. The hairs on the nape of her neck lifted as a sensation of déjà vu passed over her. This victim's condition mirrored that of the teenage girl who had suffered a cardiac arrest a couple of weeks earlier.

Quickly she detached the lead wire that monitored his vital signs from the paramedics' portable monitor and attached them to the screen built into the wall above the stretcher. "What happened?"

"His mother went to wake him for school and found him unconscious and barely breathing."

"Does she have any clue what happened?"

"She said he went to a party last night. She found a couple of pills on his beside table, but she had no idea what they were."

"You bring them in?"

"Mom did. She's in the waiting room. She's inconsolable."

"How long was he down?"

"Four, five minutes. Could have been longer. By the time we got to the scene, he'd gone into full cardiac arrest."

Elle bit her bottom lip. Not an encouraging sign. The longer a patient went without oxygen the less likely he was to survive a cardiac arrest. She stuck a device on Travis's finger that monitored the oxygen saturation level in his blood. She looked over at the screen. Ninety-two percent oxygen perfusion.

"I'm in," Jenny sang out once she had gotten the IV needle in the teenager's veins.

"Run the saline wide open," Elle said.

"Administer Desocan," said a commanding voice from the doorway.

Elle turned to see a grim-faced Dante striding purposefully into the room. Desocan was a new medication used to counteract the effect of designer drugs. Because of its many adverse side effects, the antidote drug was rarely used unless there was an absolute certainty the patient had ingested a chemically engineered designer drug. Was Dante that certain?

"We don't routinely stock Desocan," she said.

"We do now," Dante replied with a proprietary air. "I had the pharmacy order it."

Elle frowned. "The emergency room is my domain." If he'd wanted a specialized drug he should have cleared it with her before authorizing the pharmacy to spend money on something they might never use.

"He's my patient," Dante said coldly, the expression on his face brooking no argument.

This wasn't the time or place to dispute the man. Travis Russell was in serious straits and her patients always came first. Elle clamped her mouth shut and moved to relieve Heather, who she could tell was getting fatigued from giving the chest compressions.

Jenny pushed the Desocan Dante had told her to administer into the patient's IV. The paramedic turned the Ambu bag over to the respiratory therapist. The team worked in perfect unison, trying their best to save Travis Russell's life.

Just when Elle thought it was a lost cause, his heart rate blipped onto the monitor screen in normal sinus rhythm and he began breathing on his own.

A cheer went up from the medical personnel gathered in the room.

It was only then that Elle realized how tense she'd been. The muscles along her shoulders were bunched tight. Her hands were aching from repeatedly pressing against the boy's sternum. Her knees trembled. Her stomach burned. Codes, especially on children and young people, took a lot out of the entire staff.

One of the paramedics clapped Dante on the back.

"Way to go, Doc. I thought the kid was a goner for sure. Good call with the Desocan."

"Thanks," Dante said and glanced at Elle. "Get him to ICU, stat. I'm going to go talk with his family, then I'll head upstairs to write admission orders. Oh, and draw blood for a complete drug screen."

Elle nodded at her nurses—they knew what to do for the patient—and then she followed Dante out into the work lane.

"What prompted you to give the boy Desocan?" she asked.

He shrugged. "His mother brought him in last week to have a ganglion cyst removed from his wrist. The kid was in good health, but Travis bragged about partying a lot and that concerned me. From his presenting symptoms and knowing about his personal history, I feared a drug overdose. Since his condition was so dire, I was willing to gamble on adverse reactions in hopes of saving his life. It was a lucky call. Now we just have to figure out what drugs he ingested."

His explanation was perfectly rational, but it didn't stop Elle's imagination from running wild. It seemed as if he'd known for certain that Travis Russell had taken something that Desocan counteracted. But how could he know that?

Unless...

No. The off-the-wall thought that popped into her head was too preposterous to entertain.

"There's something you're not telling me," she accused and laid her hands on her hips.

He didn't say anything for a long moment, and then finally in a low tone, he said, "Patient-doctor confidentiality is a sacred thing."

"Not if it affects the kind of care we give him," she said.

His brow knit in a frown. "Follow my orders and he'll get the right care."

She didn't like his answer and she had a strong impulse to report his arrogant attitude. But who would she report him to?

Definitely not Mark.

That left only Butler and Covey, who were Mark's business partners. And what would she say? Dr. Nash knows something about his patient's private life that could influence the teenager's care, but he's not willing to share? They would back Dante up one hundred percent. Confidential Rejuvenations's reputation was built on discretion.

"Anything else, Nurse Kingston?"

"No," she mumbled.

"If that's all then, I've got to talk to his mother." He straightened and headed toward the E.D. waiting room.

Elle went back to examination room three to help Jenny and Heather get the Russell kid ready to transport up to the ICU. Once the nurses wheeled him toward the elevator, Elle remained behind to tidy up the room and make sure nothing had been forgotten.

She picked up supplies that had been taken from the cabinet but not used. There was an extra vial of Desocan. She unlocked the drug cabinet to return it to the shelf, but what she saw stopped her in her tracks.

There was ten times the amount of Desocan a hospital like Confidential Rejuvenations would use in a year. She counted the stock once, twice, three times and came up with the same number all three times. Seventy-three vials, plus the one in her hand.

For the remainder of the day, one disturbing question kept circling her brain. Why had the enigmatic Dr. Nash ordered such a large stash of Desocan?

It was as if he were expecting an epidemic.

THE MINUTE DANTE walked into the emergency room and had seen Travis Russell laid out on the stretcher, he'd known the teenager was having an adverse reaction to Rapture. But he'd had to keep quiet in case anyone in that room was involved in the manufacturing and/or distribution of the deadly designer drug.

And that included Elle.

After having assessed Travis from head to toe and written admission orders for the boy's care in the ICU, he returned to his office and paced from one wall to the other. His actions were being watched. Of that he had no doubts.

Elle already suspected him, or so he feared. She called him out on the use of Desocan. The medication was used for only one thing, and that was to counteract the detrimental affects of designer drugs. By saving Travis's life, and asking the pharmacy to stock the emergency room with Desocan, had he blown his cover?

This wasn't the first time the altruistic physician in him had warred with the justice-seeking FBI agent. His two careers were frequently at odds. In his heart, he was first and foremost a compassionate healer.

But in his head, in the dark places of his mind, he was a crusading enforcer, sworn to uphold the law.

He had to talk to his boss, Carl Briggins, and share his thoughts, but he couldn't do it here. Dante had no idea if his office was bugged. He didn't think Mark suspected him of anything, but he couldn't be too cautious.

"Hailey," he said to the receptionist as he went past the front desk. "I'm going out to my car for something. Could you give me a few minutes before my next appointment?"

"Sure, Dr. D." Hailey smiled brilliantly. The office staff had taken to calling him Dr. D. He didn't really like it. The moniker was too damned intimate. He wasn't comfortable with intimate.

Dante slipped out the side door, cell phone in hand, and hit speed dial the minute he was inside the Porsche. After asking Briggins's secretary to route him through, Dante waited for his superior officer to come on the line. He admired the older man who'd taught him the nitty-gritty of police work, but Dante had ethical problems with the deception involved in undercover assignments.

"Whatcha got for me, Nash?" Briggins asked when he came on the line.

"Sir, I'm afraid you were wrong."

"Whadaya mean? Are you calling me to tell me there's no illegal designer-street-drug ring operating out of Confidential Rejuvenations?"

How Dante wished he could answer no. Instead he said, "You were right about that. There is something fishy going on around here."

Carl Briggins's triumphant grunt said what his words did not—*I knew it.*

"But you were wrong about me," Dante explained, restlessly drumming his fingers on the dashboard.

"Come again?"

"I'm not the man for this job."

"Yes, you are."

"No, I'm not. I hate this secretive crap. I want to catch Gambezi, but not this way."

"What happened? You lose a patient?"

"Almost," Dante admitted.

"Shake it off."

"Excuse me?"

"You heard me. Shake it off. Yeah, you're feeling like a ratfink bastard spying on your old pal Lawson, but so what? If this guy is involved in what we think he's involved in, it's your duty to catch him."

"Agreed, but…"

"It's your first undercover assignment," Briggins soothed. "A case of the jitters is perfectly understandable. You won't buckle, Nash. I have complete faith in you."

"It's not that, sir."

"What is it?"

Dante hesitated.

"Uh-oh," Briggins said. "Silence isn't good. Talk to me, Nash."

"I think I'm in danger of blowing my cover."

"Are you falling for a woman?" Briggins asked.

"No," Dante said, but he felt as if he was lying. "It's nothing like that."

"Is she a suspect?"

"No."

"Wrong answer. Everyone is a suspect until proven clean. Your automatic inclination was to protect her. Not good."

"I know. That's what I'm trying to tell you."

"What's her name?"

"Elle Kingston," he admitted. "She's Lawson's ex-wife."

"You sure you're not falling for her?"

"Absolutely not. But I think she might be on to me."

"What makes you believe that?"

Briefly, Dante told him what had transpired in the emergency room with Travis Russell.

"It sounds like you covered your tracks. I'm sure you're in the clear."

"I hate lying."

"It's part of the job."

"I think someone with more undercover experience could do better."

"You want Gambezi to keeping doing to other girls what he did to your sister?"

Dante's fingers tightened around the cell phone. Briggins knew just how to land a stinging sucker punch. "No, which is why I think another officer would do better. If I screw this up, Gambezi will go underground and we'll never nail him."

"We can't introduce a new player into the game at this point. It was risky enough sliding you in there, although your history with Lawson greased the wheels. We won't have that advantage with a new agent."

"What if I fail?"

"Then you fail. But you're not going to fail. You think I would have sent you in there if I don't have complete confidence in you? This is your first covert assignment. You won't cave, Nash."

"Sir, I…"

"That's all you've got for me?"

"So far, yes. My main goal has been to establish myself here and gain Lawson's trust."

"That's exactly what you should be doing. Hang in there. It's all going to be worth it when we plant Gambezi's ugly mug behind bars."

He knew Briggins was right. Had known it before he made the call, but this duplicity was wearing. And he was worried what Elle might think of him.

*Elle.*

Was that the real source of his self-doubt? Deep inside did he fear she could somehow be mixed up in all this?

He snapped his cell phone closed just as Mark came scurrying out the side exit, his face tight with concern as he made a beeline for his Ferrari parked three cars away from where Dante was sitting. Without looking around, Mark slid behind the wheel and peeled out of the parking lot.

Something was up.

Should he follow him?

He glanced in the direction of his office, knowing he had a waiting room full of patients. Before he could decide whether pursuing Mark was worth the risk, Hailey pushed through the front doors of the office building, heading straight toward him.

Dante got out to meet her. "What is it?"

"Pete Russell's on the phone."

"Pete Russell?" Dante's mind wasn't tracking her conversation. He was still wondering where Mark had gone so quickly and what he was up to in the middle of a workday.

"You know, Pete Russell," she said. "Travis Russell's dad and Austin's hottest musician. He's calling to thank you for saving Travis's life and to invite the entire staff of Confidential Rejuvenations to a private party at his house next Friday night." Hailey took his arm, effectively ending any lingering thoughts he had of following Mark. "Come on. Hurry, before he hangs up."

# 5

DANTE ARRIVED AT THE Russells' lavish home on the out-
skirts of Austin sometime after eleven o'clock. He had
forgone the concert, knowing there would be no chance
for eavesdropping or investigating in that venue.

A line of valets hustled to park the expensive vehicles
crawling up the driveway in front of him. He waited his
turn, watching the well-dressed guests as they exited their
vehicles, tossed car keys to the valets and then swept up
the stone walkway to the Texas-sized mansion.

Feeling decidedly out of place, Dante pasted a fake
smile on his lips, passed the valet a big tip and followed
the crowd inside. He didn't see anyone he knew, so he
made a beeline for the buffet table, where he could at least
pretend to be engrossed with the food while slipping sur-
reptitious glances at the crowd.

But he didn't make it that far.

Before he was halfway across the room, he heard Mark
call out to him. "Dante!"

He spied his ex-roommate coming toward him with a
beautiful young woman hooked to his arm. He'd seen the
woman's face plastered across billboards and movie posters,
but he'd never seen a Cassandra Roberts film, although he
did attend many other kinds of movies when his demanding work schedule allowed it. She was arrestingly gorgeous

with her long, blond hair and large doe-eyes, but she seemed somehow vacant and lost. Mark had traded Elle, a vibrant, substantial woman, for this vacuous creature?

The fool.

"Hey, man, glad to see you made it." Mark clapped him on the shoulder.

"Wouldn't miss it."

Cassandra delicately cleared her throat.

"Oh," Mark said, and draped his arm around Cassandra's waist. "This is my wife, Cassandra. Cass, this is my old college roommate, Dante Nash."

Dante shook Cassandra's hand at the very same moment he looked across the room and saw Elle standing in the corner, a martini glass clutched in her hand. She looked as if she'd just been slapped across the face.

"Nice to meet you," he murmured, but his eyes were on Elle.

Quickly she pivoted and slipped out of the room. It was all he could do to keep himself from going after her.

"Do you think I could have a word with you in private?" Mark asked.

"Sure."

"Oh, no," Cassandra whined. "Don't tell me you're going to talk business."

Mark kissed his wife on the cheek. "Sorry, darling, it pays the bills. I'm sure your adoring public won't mind keeping you entertained for a few minutes."

Cassandra pretended to pout until Mark leaned over and whispered something in her ear that made her giggle. "I'm going to hold you to that," she said, and then drifted off to talk to someone she knew.

Mark inclined his head. "Let's take a walk outside."

As they pushed through the throng, heading for an exit,

Dante caught sight of Elle again. She was at the buffet table talking to Dr. Vanessa Rodriquez. But as he and Mark passed by, she turned her head and caught his eye.

The air in the room suddenly seemed to quiver with her sexuality, beckoning him forward. She did not smile. Neither did Dante. He placed a palm on the back of his neck, dropped his gaze, nodded to Mark, pretending he was listening.

But his mind was completely preoccupied with Elle.

He slipped another look in her direction. She was still watching him. She wore an emerald-green halter dress made from some kind of silky material that clung provocatively to her curves. His fingers itched to reach up and untie that dress and watch it fall. Buffering waves of sexual attraction shimmered across the space between them like summer heat rising up off fresh asphalt.

"This way," Mark said, breaking Dante's train of thought.

Reluctantly, he pried his eyes off Elle. He had to remember why he was here and what was at stake.

They went out the back door and walked past a group of smokers huddled on the patio, taking long drags off their cigarettes. The night was perfect. Full moon, lots of stars, balmy breeze. Too bad Dante was in no frame of mind to enjoy it.

"Let's go down to the fishing dock."

"You've been here before?" Dante asked.

"Pete and Cassandra are old friends."

"Ah," he said. "Did they used to be lovers?"

"I don't ask her those kinds of questions," Mark said. "What she did before me is none of my concern."

"She's a beautiful girl," he said.

"I'm a lucky man."

"What about Elle?" Dante asked.

"What about her?"

"She's beautiful, too."

"Come on, buddy." Mark gave a half laugh, half snort. "You're talking the difference between meatloaf and filet mignon."

Dante had an urge to pop Mark in the mouth with his fist. He thought Cassandra was filet mignon? To Dante's way of thinking, Elle was the prime cut and Cassandra was nothing more than a blond rice cake.

The grass was damp underneath their feet as they walked the quarter mile down a rolling hill below the house to a redwood dock overlooking a fishing pond. There was no one else around. The full moon cast a glow of light across the still water. The air smelled earthy.

Mark leaned his backside against the railing, crossed his arms over his chest and grinned at Dante the way he had on the football field at UT whenever they won a close game. Mark had been the first-string quarterback and Dante his favorite wide receiver. Together they'd led their team to a Cotton Bowl victory during their senior year.

"I'm glad you came to Confidential Rejuvenations. It's like old times. Only with a lot more money. Remember how good we were on the gridiron?"

Dante nodded. "I do."

"A well-oiled precision team. When we were on the field, it was as if we could read each other's mind."

"Yes."

"We both had drive and ambition, both of us running away from our ugly childhoods, both of us running toward success as fast as we could."

What Mark said was true enough. Their traumatic pasts had been the magnet that had drawn them together. The football field had been the thing that bonded them. Yet in spite of all they had in common, their interests had not made them fast friends. Their outlooks on life were polar opposites, their core values too different.

Dante truly believed in helping others. In his heart, he'd always known Mark merely paid lip service to the concept. Only three things motivated Mark Lawson—money, prestige and women.

"We could be like that again."

"What do you mean?"

"A team, like we were in college."

"Isn't that what we are now?"

Mark shook his head.

Dante tensed. His body went on full alert. "I'm not following you."

Mark didn't answer immediately. Dante could tell he was weighing his words before he spoke. A fish broke the water of the pond, jumping up to catch a june bug buzzing around the dock light. There was a flopping sound, followed by a smacking splash as the fish sank back underneath the surface.

"Big one," Mark commented, and nodded at the widening ripples.

Dante leaned over the rail, watching the waves spread out across the pond. "Uh-huh."

"You do much fishing?"

He had no idea where this conversation was headed, but he knew they weren't really talking about fish. "Not much."

"It's all about the bait."

"The bait?"

"Different kinds of fish like different kinds of bait. Lures work great for bass. Crappies like minnow. Perch go for worms. But catfish? They'll hit anything."

Dante met Mark's gaze. "Who knew?"

"Exactly."

They stood looking at each other. Was Mark on to him? Was that what was going on here? Or was it something else? He had to be careful. "So you fish a lot."

"For relaxation."

"Ah," Dante said. "I never pegged you for a fisherman."

The tension was like a tightrope. Dante could feel it under his skin, like rubber bands twisted to the snapping point. Neither of them said anything for the longest moment. Frogs croaked. Crickets chirped. The breeze gusted. From the house came the distant sound of laughter and music. It felt as far away as the moon. Neither one of them took their eyes off the other.

Mark cleared his throat.

Dante curled his fingers into his palms. *We're getting down to it now.* Whatever "it" was.

"I've noticed you could use some relaxation. You work too hard, Dante. You always have."

*And you've always taken the easy way out.*

"You need to loosen up. For your own mental health. You can't be an effective doctor without a little R & R."

Where was Mark headed with this? "You've got a point," Dante conceded.

"Know what I do when stress gets to me?"

"Fish?"

Mark laughed. "Fishing's good but a little dull, if you know what I mean."

"I hear you."

"You ever try anything to take the edge off?" Mark asked.

"You mean like pharmaceuticals?"

His smile widened. "I definitely mean pharmaceuticals."

Dante swallowed hard as the magnitude of the moment hit him. Mark was on the verge of telling him about Rapture. He couldn't act too eager. He had to make this look realistic. "You got a special pill that works for you?"

"You ever take Viagra?"

"Never needed any."

"Not from need, but for recreation. Believe me when I tell you the stuff greatly enhances sexual pleasure."

"Does it?"

"Ever done any Ecstasy?"

"Hey, man, you said it yourself. I've been working too hard to play."

"Well, things are about to change for you my friend. You are about to have the experience of a lifetime." Mark reached into his pocket and pulled out a thin oblong yellow pill.

Sharp-edged excitement chewed on Dante along with anger and disappointment. He had wanted to give Mark the benefit of the doubt that he was not involved with Furio Gambezi and the manufacturing of illegal designer drugs. But the sick feeling in the pit of his stomach told him that such a belief was a fairy tale. "What's this?"

"Rapture. It's a euphoric libido enhancer that produces the ultimate sexual high. It has the stiffening and staying power of Viagra, with the heightened sensory awareness of Ecstasy. It's like Tantric sex in a tablet. You can stay hard and horny and go at it for days. Cassandra loves it. They can't get enough of the stuff in Hollywood."

Dante looked from the pill in Mark's open palm to the measured expression in his eyes. "Is it a prescription drug?"

"No."

"Where did you get it?"

"I have my sources."

"That sounds mysterious."

"Give it a try. I promise you won't regret it," Mark said, admitting nothing.

The urge to double up his fist and smack his old roommate in the mouth was so strong it was all Dante could do to restrain himself. He kept thinking of Leeza, destroyed by drugs and her association with Furio Gambezi.

His and Mark's eyes locked.

This was too easy. Here was Mark willingly sharing his illicit secret. Dante didn't trust "easy." It could be a trap. His cover could have been blown; the pill laced with poison, and this was Mark's way of getting rid of him.

"Take it," Mark said, his words a command, not a request. "And then go enjoy the party. Tomorrow, you call me up and tell me what you think. If we're of like minds about this product, I could have a very lucrative business proposition for you."

"Manufacturing this drug?"

Mark gave a noncommittal shrug, but his eyes said, *Hell yes.*

A chill shot up Dante's spine. So that was it. Mark was looking for a business partner. Dante was smart enough to understand why. Mark needed a scapegoat to blame the whole thing on if things went south.

The irony was so sweet Dante almost laughed. Mark had unwittingly picked the undercover FBI agent for his pigeon. With this kind of luck, he'd have the case wrapped up by Monday.

"By the way, you're going to be needing this." Mark reached inside his jacket, drew out a three-pack of condoms and slipped them into the front pocket of Dante's shirt.

"Now down the hatch." Mark looked meaningfully at the pill in Dante's hand.

Realizing he was sealing his fate, but knowing there was no way he could refuse at this point, Dante popped the pill into his mouth and swallowed.

COSMOPOLITAN IN HAND, Elle stood with her friends in the middle of Pete Russell's family room. One of Pete's music videos was playing on all of the big-screen plasma television sets scattered throughout the house. The place was noisier than downtown Austin on New Year's Eve. Elle could barely hear her own thoughts.

Across the room, Cassandra Roberts was talking to the Lieutenant Governor of Texas. Over in the corner, four Dallas Cowboys dominated the foosball table. Near the fireplace a colorful local mystery writer was knocking back shooters of butterscotch schnapps with a Pulitzer-prizewinning journalist. The party was a veritable who's who of Confidential Rejuvenations's patient list.

Elle, accustomed to celebrity, was not impressed. She knew what these people looked like with their clothes off. That was one thing about being a nurse—you learned pretty quickly illness and death didn't play favorites. VIPs got sick just like everyone else. Their celebrity status couldn't protect them from the inevitable.

"What's at the back door?" Julie shouted above the music.

"Huh?" Elle blinked.

"You keep staring at the back door."

"Do I?" Elle shouted back.

"Yes, you do," Vanessa confirmed. "You seem very distracted."

"It's the loud music that's distracting." Elle waved a hand at the surround-sound-system speakers mounted in the corners.

"It's more than that." Vanessa arched an eyebrow. She

knew something was up. It wasn't easy pulling anything over on Vanessa.

"Okay," Elle admitted. "I saw Mark ditch Cassandra and leave the party with Dante."

"So?" Vanessa shrugged. "Why should you care?"

"I don't care," Elle said, knowing she was lying. She did care about Dante and she was afraid that he was getting too chummy with her ex. Did he have any idea what Mark was capable of? "I'm just wondering what Mark is up to, that's all."

"You've got to stop thinking about him, Elle." Julie linked an arm through hers. "Here, let's look around the room and see if we can find you a red-hot celebrity stud to go home with."

"I don't want a red-shot stud." And she certainly didn't want to go home with a celebrity.

Just then the back door opened and Mark sauntered in. Elle darted a glance behind her ex-husband. No sign of Dante. Disappointment settled over her and she realized she'd been waiting here just to see him. What was it about that man that so intrigued her? Hadn't she had enough of doctors?

"Oooh," Julie said. "Looks like Mark is coming over. You want we should scatter?"

Elle grabbed Julie's forearm with her free hand, her cosmopolitan balanced in the other. "Don't you dare leave me alone with him."

Mark's smile was patently false. She had come to recognize that artificial smile for exactly what it was—a tool. He wanted something from her. Every muscle in Elle's body tensed.

"Hello, Ell-evator," he greeted her with the goofy name he'd called her when they were dating.

"What do you want?" she snapped.

"Can't a guy just stop by and say hi to his ex-wife?" He rounded his eyes, trying to look innocent. She knew that look and she wasn't falling for it.

"Not when that guy is you."

"You've got to get over your bitterness, babe. It'll age you prematurely." He canted his head. "Is that a new wrinkle on your forehead?"

Elle wanted so badly to fling her drink in his smug face, but she refused to rise to his taunts. She wouldn't give him the satisfaction of knowing that he'd gotten to her.

"What do you want?" she reiterated through clenched teeth. How in the world had she ever thought she loved this man?

*He had you fooled. He's a consummate actor. He even had your family fooled and they're all cops. You can't blame yourself.*

But she did.

She loved too easily and with all her heart. And she was loyal to the bone, never giving up on those she'd loved until they pushed her to extremes.

Loving and loyal.

Her best qualities, or so people told her. Yeah, right. For her, loving loyalty had been a trap, blinding her to Mark's flaws, which she should have seen. She'd sworn to herself she wouldn't be so stupid in the future. No more loving easily or blindly. No more making a fool of herself over a man.

Mark leaned in close. Too close. His hand brushed hers, the one holding the drink. He pressed his lips to her ear. "It's time to loosen up, Ell-evator."

Elle refused to shudder, to show any reaction at all. She wouldn't give him the satisfaction. What in the hell was he talking about? Why was he over here bothering her when she could see Cassandra across the room shooting daggers with her glare?

"Your new wife's giving you the evil eye," Elle said. "Better be a good boy and scurry on over before she takes away your Rolex."

"Bitchy," Mark whispered. "Looks like you haven't had enough to drink yet. Bottoms up." Then he turned and walked toward Cassandra.

It was only then Elle realized she'd been holding her breath. Anger coursed through her. She had no idea what her ex was up to or what he was trying to pull other than to rattle her cage.

Bastard.

Hand trembling, she raised the cosmo to her lips and knocked back the vodka-soaked drink. The liquid hit her tongue with a sharp, acrid taste and she'd already gulped down more than half of it before she recognized the taste was off.

Wrinkling her nose, she wiped her palm across her mouth and shivered against the bitter flavor. That was the worst cosmo she'd ever tasted. She set the remainder of the drink on a nearby table.

"What was that all about?" Vanessa asked her.

Elle shook her head. "I have no idea. He's just being a jerk-off I guess. Yuck, that drink was terrible. I'm going after something else to get the taste of it out of my mouth. You guys want anything from the bar?"

"I'm good to go." Julie held up a full glass of white wine.

"I'm not drinking," Vanessa said. "On call all weekend."

Elle nodded and made a beeline for the bar. Her impulse was to get drunk enough to forget about Mark, but by the time she'd stood in line for another drink her mood had changed. Suddenly she was feeling very warm and mellow inside. The cosmo might have tasted awful, but it had quickly gone to her head. Instead of ordering another drink, she simply asked for a glass of water; her mouth had suddenly gone bone-dry.

She took her water and turned away from the bar. A rolling heat started at the top of her head and oozed all the way down her body to lodge tightly in her groin. Sweet rippling waves of sensation washed over her. Her entire body felt tingly hot. Her breasts ached and her nipples beaded.

No beating around the bush, she was straight-up horny. Everything seemed to blur in a timeless haze. She drifted around the room giddy and dazed. Wow. What had been in that drink?

The room was aglow with color. Everyone was so good-looking. All around her couples were talking and touching and kissing. The pounding tempo of her heart joined the throbbing beat of the music. She felt smooth and liquid and primal. The erotic sensation pulsated through every cell in her body.

Growing, escalating, swelling.

Her gaze traveled around the room. From man to man. She stared at hips and butts and broad shoulders and flat chests. She licked her lips. What was it Julie had said about picking up a red-hot stud and taking him home with her? What was it Vanessa had suggested about a wild affair with a rebound guy to cleanse Mark from her palate? The idea held extraordinary appeal.

Yes. That's exactly what she was going to do. Have sex with the next gorgeous man she laid eyes on and forget all about her stupid ex-husband.

And that was when she spied Dante.

DANTE STAGGERED INTO the party, teeth clenched against the erotic sensations assaulting him at every turn. His body was on fire with desire. The Rapture he'd swallowed dulling his brain, scorching his body and hardening his cock, making him feel thunderously out of control.

Every sensation was magnified, amplified, exaggerated.

He needed a woman and he needed one now.

No, no. He was not going to give into the drug. He was strong. He could fight this.

But not when Elle Kingston was headed straight toward him, a provocative smile curling her full raspberry-colored lips. Those devastating lips.

He wanted to taste them, feel the rush of her breath. She had the most incredible mouth. The swell of the lower lip, the shapely arch of the upper and the sweet territory in between where the glossy satin of her pout yielded to the silky, moist secrets of her tongue.

God, she was beautiful.

The emerald-green halter dress she wore accentuated the mossy green of her eyes and complimented her rich auburn hair. Her arms were bare and the swingy hem of the dress molded against her thighs as she walked.

A fresh surge of heated desire shot through his body.

Elle was smart, sexy and stubborn as hell—the three things Dante loved most in a woman.

And all he could think about was sex.

His gaze fixed on hers. He had to get inside her. Had to possess her, penetrate her, permeate her in some way. Her green eyes glistened with an illustrious sheen. Her auburn hair was a riot of curls around her interesting face.

Elle Kingston's face.

Those feminine cheekbones, the generous mouth, the

eyes that told him she was more woman than he could handle. Ever since he'd arrived at Confidential Rejuvenations he'd imagined making love to her in a hundred different ways but he'd never intended on acting on those impulses.

Until now.

*It's the Rapture. You can't make love to her, no matter how badly you might want to. You're under the effects of a mind-altering—*

She licked her lips and he totally lost his train of thought.

When had she gotten so deeply under his skin? This sort of thing didn't happen to Dante. He was aloof, self-contained and largely unaffected by romantic feelings.

But that was all gone now.

*Rapture. It's the Rapture.*

"Hello, Dante," Elle murmured when she was close enough to be heard over the loud music.

"Elle." It was all he could say. No more words came from his mouth.

"I want to be with you," she said.

He didn't question it. Right now, in his addled state of mind, it made perfect sense.

"I want to be with you, too."

They looked into each other's eyes, their meaning clear. If the room hadn't been packed with people he would have torn her clothes off right then and there.

"Where can we go?" she asked.

"Come on." He took her hand. "We'll find a place."

Her hand felt thin and fragile in his, as if she might break. A sudden rush of tenderness swept through him and he had the strangest urge to scoop her into his arms and carry her away.

He pulled her through the house, past movie stars and

musicians, past groupies and hangers-on. They weren't the only ones looking for a make-out spot. They were almost running as they tried locked bedroom door after locked bedroom door.

"Hurry, hurry," she urged him. "I need you."

He was frantic. She was frantic. It was crazy, wild. He'd never felt anything like it. In his drugged state, her desperation did not seem odd. It matched Dante's own flaming desire.

*Outside,* he thought. When Mark had taken him out to the lake, he'd seen a two-story garage at the side of the house.

"Come on," he said, and led her out the back entrance.

They stumbled outside into the darkness, past couples kissing on the patio, past the hot tub where guests sat in whirling water, past the swaying cottonwood trees, leaves rustling in the breeze. The air was rich with the smell of honeysuckle and fresh-mown grass. The lights were out in the garage. They approached the side door. Dante prayed it wasn't locked.

The door opened at his touch and swung inward.

He flicked on the lights and closed the door behind them. The four-car garage housed a Bentley, a Hummer, two Harley-Davidson motorcycles and a Cadillac Escalade. Nowhere to make love here unless they crawled into the back of a vehicle.

"Upstairs," Elle said, the desperation in her voice matching the pounding desperation in his groin. She dragged him up the stairs to the second story. They found a rumpus room with a glorious pool table just made for lust-crazed sex.

She turned into him. Her breasts pressed against his bicep. She lifted her head to meet his eyes. He splayed a palm against her lower back.

Her belly was pressed flat against the waistband of his pants. She had to feel his hard-on; there was no way she could miss it. He could certainly feel her belly trembling and her nipples stiffening.

She snaked her arms around his neck. "Make love to me, Dante, make love to me now."

He wanted to be a gentleman, to double-check her intentions by asking her if this was what she really wanted. But the gentlemanly part of his brain had checked out. Fogged by passion and Rapture and Elle.

Sweet Elle.

He dipped his head.

Her gaze was fixed on his lips, begging for a kiss.

Dante moaned. He'd wanted to do this from the moment he'd first laid eyes on her. His hand crept up her spine to the nape of her neck, his fingers pushing up through the beautiful red tangle of curls.

"Please," she whimpered. "Please don't make me wait anymore."

And because he couldn't take one minute more of not being completely naked and pressed against her, bare skin to bare skin, Dante tilted her head and speared his tongue past her moist, receptive lips.

# 6

---

DANTE'S MOUTH SIZZLED against Elle's, delicious as prime rib fresh off the grill. He heated her up from the inside out. Searing her, branding her, claiming her, flash-melting the part of her that had frozen up like Iceland in February.

For one silly, illogical minute she wished they could stay fused like this together forever. His heat warming her heart, nurturing her soul in the way that it ached to be nurtured.

He kissed her. Hard and hot and deep.

His grip tightened around her, pulling her close, holding her against him. She melted into him like caramel and hot fudge. Her eyelids drifted closed. Her knees quivered. She floated along, dazzled and dizzy. It felt like the most natural thing in the entire world.

Explicit pictures flashed through her brain in a montage of moving snapshots. His naked body, stretched out over hers. His penis big and hard for her. She, helpless and vulnerable and writhing with pleasure.

She wanted him so badly it terrified her.

Her fingers were tangled in the silk of his hair and she was holding him in place, loath to let him go, her heart pounding in a brilliant timpani of sound and color. Yes, color. The beat of her heart was pink and fresh and new. The taste of it like cotton candy mixed with sin. She could feel her pulse, hear it, see it, taste it and smell it in a strange kaleidoscope of sensation.

She had no idea how this was possible. It was as if Dante's mouth was some kind of mind-altering drug and she was helpless to resist.

Obviously something was wrong with her. She wasn't thinking straight. Her brain was askew, her conscience and common sense washed away by the rush of adrenaline pushing through her veins.

Dante shifted, changing the tilt of his head. He lightened the kiss, turning it into a seductive tease, using the suction of his mouth to tug at her bottom lip. His tongue flicked tenderly against hers. A shower of hot, soft kisses trailed from her lips, down her chin to the underside of her throat. And when he moved up to nibble her earlobe, her entire body shuddered against his.

She heard a soft sound of pleasure escape her lips as she sighed into him.

He slid a hand up her spine until his palm grazed the bare skin exposed by her halter dress. His fingers fanned.

She shivered against him in spite of the warmth his hand generated. Shivered from delight and anticipation. She'd been lusting after him for weeks and secretly fantasizing about such a moment as this. She never wanted it to end.

And they were just getting started.

Her hand trembled, drunk and woozy, and she was grateful to have him to lean into. Chest to chest, thigh to thigh and every glorious body part in between.

This wasn't her. This wanton feeling of free fall, but she loved it, reveled in it. What was happening? She didn't know. Didn't care that her head was spinning and her heart was chugging and her lips were burning.

He increased the pressure, his tongue hungry and insistent.

She moaned again, an urgent, helpless sound that shocked, delighted and escalated her arousal all at the same time. She was electrified.

Oh yes, yes, this feeling…this…this… She had no word for what it was. She'd never felt it before. Every muscle in her body was outrageously alive, every square inch of her skin crying out for more, more, more of his touch.

Then Dante pulled back.

Elle whimpered. "No."

He stared into her eyes.

Their gazes locked and they were both breathing in rapid, rhythmic gasps.

Slowly he reached out to run a knuckle over her cheek-bone. His eyes were murky with desire. His body was tensed as if he was barely able to control himself.

"What is it?" she whispered.

He swallowed. She could feel the steel of his erection straining the zipper of his chinos.

"Are you sure you really, really want this?"

"I've never wanted anything more."

The words, spoken in the quiet of the garage, sounded certain but strangely vulnerable. She felt it in the very core of her body. She *was* vulnerable. Vulnerable and desperate and hungry for masculine attention. And she wasn't one bit ashamed of her need.

This was pathetic.

She should tell him no, that she'd changed her mind. But her body was tingling and her blood was churning and she wanted him so very, very badly, and the moist aching between her legs was almost more than she could bear.

He took her at her word and before she even knew what

he was doing, he'd scooped her off her feet and carried her over to the pool table. His strength, the lusty look in his eyes, left her feeling utterly feminine.

She was on her back on the green felt. On the wall to one side was a rack of pool cues. A batch of colorful balls encased in a beige plastic triangle rested on a nearby credenza along with several little cubes of chalk. An oblong florescent light hung suspended over the table.

Dante was climbing up beside her, kicking off his shoes and wrestling off his jacket as he went. He tossed it off into a corner.

Elle looked up into his eyes and the room spun like a warm, beautiful carousel.

He planted one knee on either side of her hips, loomed over her, and looked down at her. He was pure animal.

His big size made her feel small but not delicate. In fact, she felt empowered. She had reduced this big man to this. She'd claimed his control.

His smell was spicy and masculine—the zestiness of soap, the woodsy scent of pine, the richness of leather. She wanted to bury her nose against his salty skin again and inhale him.

A thrill unlike anything she'd ever experienced galloped through her. She moistened her dry lips with a flick of her tongue. All these years and she'd never felt so desired.

He leaned down. Slowly.

Her heart thumped.

He dipped his head lower and pushed it to the throbbing, flushing pulse at the hollow of her neck. "How's that feel?" he asked.

With his hot mouth against her bare skin, she could scarcely draw in air much less speak. "Awesome," she managed to whisper.

He chuckled and the sound filled her with a soft, round pleasure. She realized then she'd never heard him laugh. *She* had made him laugh. Elle felt at once both powerful and incredibly sexy. It was an unaccustomed feeling.

Dante kissed her on the forehead, sweetly, tenderly. Why was he kissing her on the forehead? She wanted him to ravage her with his tongue. Wanted him to take her down to depths where she'd never been before. Wanted it dark and hard and dirty.

Then his naughty hand was slipping up her inner thigh, reaching for her thong panties.

Elle arched her hips and stared up into his eyes, reached out and took hold of his shoulders with both hands. He peeled off the thin strip of silk and lace, slowly dragging it down her legs, the material rubbing erotically over her skin as he skimmed the panties past her knees and down her calves.

He tossed the panties away. They landed in the netherworld with his jacket. To Elle, anything beyond the pool table no longer existed.

His fingers were back on her thighs. His thumb gently tracing circles.

A new sensation gripped her. Her body twitched involuntarily and she dropped her knees, giving him easier access to the most sacred, secret part of her.

She hadn't been with a man since her divorce. Hadn't wanted to be with one until now. And somehow, he had washed away the memories of her mistakes and Elle felt as if she was starting out bright and shiny new.

Madonna's "Like A Virgin" ran through her head, because that's what it was like, as if she was being touched by a man for the very first time in her life.

Unfurling, opening, blooming, blossoming, the past was gone. There was only now. Only Dante.

He pushed the hem of her dress up to her waist and kneed her legs apart.

She gasped at the suddenness of it, at the coolness of the air against her heated skin.

He rocked back on his heels, dropped his gaze and an incredibly sexy noise slipped from his lips. She felt her nipples tighten at the sound of it.

"Beautiful," he murmured. "So beautiful."

"My turn," she said, surprised at her own boldness, making demands. "I want to see something beautiful, too."

She sat up and reached for the buttons of his dress shirt. She worked them open one by one, revealing more and more of him.

He was as gorgeous as she'd anticipated. Hard-muscled chest. Flat, taut abs. Not the body of your average surgeon. Much more like a warrior or a cop.

The thrilling sight of his bare chest raised chill bumps up her forearms.

Dante finished the job for her. Tugging his shirt from his waistband, unbuckling his belt, shucking off his pants like a man on a serious mission.

Then something fell from his shirt pocket and hit the table with a soft plop.

Both their eyes tracked the movement. Elle saw the condoms and she looked up to meet his gaze. His manly chest exposed, knees dug into the pool table on either side of her. She was sitting up between his legs, her dress hiked to her waist, panties missing. Talk about a compromising position.

Elle arched her eyebrows. "Looking to get lucky tonight?"

"No…I…"

"Do you always carry condoms in your shirt pocket?"

Damn if his cheeks didn't tinge pink. He was blushing. She found it endearing. Elle smiled. "It's okay. I'm glad that you're prepared because I'm not. I'm out of my head and I'm glad for it."

"I don't want you to think that…"

"Don't think," she said. "I don't want to think. I like this not-thinking thing. Let's not think together. Let's just feel. Come on, get naked."

"You're sure?"

"Just do me, Dante."

"Yes, ma'am."

While he disposed of his clothes, Elle reached up to undo the tie of her halter dress. It fell open, revealing that she was braless.

He took one look at her breasts and growled.

She lay back and he was upon her. Kissing her more furiously than he'd kissed her before. He kissed her lips until they stung with urgency and then he moved on, down her chin to the sensitive underside of her jaw, to the hollow of her throat until he ended up at her aching, swollen breasts.

Her body quivered.

"I've wanted you from the minute I stepped into your emergency room," he whispered.

"Really?"

"You doubt this?" He took her hand and guided it to his stiff erection.

She smiled.

"See what you do to me."

"But you never flirted with me."

"Okay, so I've never been good at the foreplay stuff," he admitted.

"I think," she said, "you underestimate yourself. I've been wet for you all evening."

"I think you don't know the truth of it."

"What does that mean?"

He got a strange look on his face, as if he'd said too much, stepped over some kind of boundary and Elle was suddenly so afraid that she'd lost him and he wouldn't make love to her. Reaching up, she wrapped her arms around his neck and pulled him down flush against her.

She slipped her fingers through his hair. Held his head still and kissed him with all the fervent intensity she had inside her.

Her body was slick for him and his body was hard for her. They just needed to get together to make this happen. To salve and soothe each other.

Elle wriggled beneath him. Dante groaned.

His penis was so big, so hard. She licked her lips. "Condom," she gasped. "Where's a condom?"

He fumbled on the table, found it.

In her desperation to have him, she snatched the condom from his hand, ripped it open with her teeth and with trembling fingers, pushed him back just long enough to roll it on for him.

"Take me now," she demanded, the lust and the urge more than she could possibly tolerate for one more minute. She had to have this man or die. The desire was in her veins, in her blood, in her brain.

Now, now, now.

He pushed inside of her. A rush of heat so overwhelming she could not breathe suffused her feminine core. Her muscles tensed around him, drawing his hard shaft in deeper.

"You are so tight." He groaned. "It feels righteous."

She couldn't answer. She'd always dreamed of sex like this. Wild and hungry and brilliantly good. But this was so much more than she'd ever bargained for.

The hard glide of his penis, his big, hot body pressing into her was a marvelous tension. With each fevered thrust she wanted more. Wanted him deeper.

Their simultaneous sounds of pleasure merged in the air.

Dante twisted his hips, rocking deeper and deeper into her softness. Her mind was mush. Images flashed through her head. Colors, sounds, sensations. Nothing had ever felt like this before. Certainly not with Mark and not with the two other lovers she'd had before him.

This was unique.

This was Dante.

It felt right. It felt perfect. It felt like the missing piece of the puzzle.

Her body tingled from the top of her head to the tips of her toes. She bucked her hips up to meet his thrusts, ran her hands over his sweat-slicked skin, dug her fingernails into his muscles.

He grew inside her until there was no space unoccupied by him. She was owned, claimed, possessed.

*Yes.*

Every other thought left her head. There was only room for him.

She wrapped her legs around his waist, miraculously pulling him deeper into her body. Blindly she grabbed for something to hold on to and her hands found the pockets on either side of the pool table. His fierce, insistent thrusts pushed her to the limits of her endurance. The green felt of the pool table burned her back. She didn't care. She relished the burn.

How could this be so glorious? This amazing? What made him so special? What made it so good between them? She felt as if she had found the golden key to the universe.

They were perfectly in tune. Linked. Locked. As if they'd known each other for centuries instead of for just a few short weeks. It was as if she'd been waiting for this man her entire life and her marriage to Mark had been nothing but a weak dress rehearsal for the real thing.

Dante seemed to know everything about her body. Where she ached to be stroked. How she liked to be kissed. He seemed to have an unerring sense of direction when it came to mapping out her erogenous zones. He heightened her senses. Left her writhing and gasping and whimpering. Yearning for more of him in wordless hunger, whimpering in a voice she barely recognized as her own.

Dante dipped his head, took one straining nipple into his mouth as he thrust relentlessly into her, giving her more of him than she could possibly stand. Her womb tightened. Her breath flew out of her.

Every ramming stroke took her higher and higher toward her ultimate goal. It was fierce, extreme, flawless. He pinned her to the pool table with his arms. Holding her, driving into her. She cried his name over and over, until tears rolled down her cheeks and sensation surmounted her.

"You're crying," he whispered and stopped moving. "Am I hurting you?"

"No, no."

"Why are you crying?"

She shook her head, unable to speak.

Dante flicked her tears away with both thumbs. "Talk to me, Elle. What's wrong?"

"Nothing…it's great," she wrenched the words from her mouth. "Or at least it was until you stopped. Don't stop. Please don't stop."

"Tears of pleasure?" He seemed confused by that. "Is that what it is?"

"Yes, yes, now come on before I stop crying and I lose the feeling."

He made a noise low in his throat and kissed the tears from her cheeks as he began moving inside her again with soft, determined strokes.

"Ah," she murmured. "That's it."

He quickened his pace, determination on his face. She watched him watching her as he filled her up all the way to her heart.

And then she just fell.

Rolling into the orgasm as if it had always been her fate. She saw stars and moons and rainbows.

She heard his groan and knew he was following her into the abyss, rocking and pumping and thrusting. He called out her name and the sound of it changed something deep inside of her forever.

DANTE LAY TREMBLING on the pool table beside Elle, his muscles spent, mind numb.

*What the hell have you done?*

He couldn't look at her. Couldn't speak. Not just from breathless exertion, but from the heavy guilt weighing down his tongue.

"Dante." She sighed and rested her forehead, damp with the sweat of their joining, against his bare chest.

Instinctively he wrapped an arm around her and she curled her body into his. His heart beat like jungle drums and his conscience ate him clean as a cannibal. How could he have let this happen?

*She asked for it. You wanted it. It felt so damned good, you just went for it.*

He clenched his right hand into a fist. No, no. This was all wrong. He should not have done this. He should not have made love to her while under the influence of Mark's mind-altering drug. It skewered everything. He could not trust what he was feeling. It was all a deception. He couldn't trust her, but most of all, he couldn't trust himself. He was dangerously close to jeopardizing his investigation.

Already he was feeling tender, vulnerable feelings he should not be feeling.

Fool.

Dante stared at the ceiling and then closed his eyes against the sweet pressure of her head on his chest. He wanted to thread his hands through her hair, lift up her face to his and kiss her again. He wanted to trace his fingers over her face, memorize every detail for future reference when he thought back on his moment. But dammit, he had no business thinking about her at all, much less making love to her.

But somehow Elle had wound her way inside his head and he didn't know how to get her out. He'd never met a woman who gave herself so fully to sex.

But it didn't feel false.

It felt stunningly real.

*Hey, it's not real. Don't fall for the trap. That's what this drug does. Sucks you in. Deceives you. Makes the impossible seem possible.*

So here was another unexpected dangerous side effect of Rapture, inexplicable feelings that didn't actually belong to him, feelings that confused and distorted reality.

Feelings that scared the hell out of a man who'd tried his damndest for so long not to feel anything more than anger and determination and revenge.

He'd screwed up.

Big time.

If he told Briggins what he'd had to do to gain Mark's trust, his boss would go ballistic. Taking illegal drugs was not what he'd signed on to do. But he'd had no choice, and he hated the circumstances that had forced him to lower his standards.

Swallowing past the lump in his throat, Dante opened his eyes. One thing was startlingly clear. He had to make sure that what had happened here tonight with Elle must not happen again.

Awkwardly, he slipped his arm out from behind her neck. She looked over at him and an emotion he couldn't name overwhelmed him. Her hair was tousled and her eyes looked so damned vulnerable, as if she too were having serious second thoughts.

"We better get out of here before someone catches us like this." Purposefully he took her by the shoulders and put her away from him so he could sit up. He saw a flash of what he took to be hurt in her eyes but it was quickly gone and he told himself he was just imagining it.

She tucked her bottom lip up between her front teeth. If she'd said one single thing to encourage him he would have kissed her again.

Dumb ass. Chump.

*Fool.*

But she didn't say anything at all, just scooted away from him, swung her legs over the side of the pool table, modestly pulling up her clothes.

He wanted to say something to her. To make this awkwardness go away, to fix things between them, but he couldn't find the right words.

And regret had him bound up like titanium twine.

"Elle—"

"Yeah?"

She peered at him as she wriggled into her panties. His dick hardened all over again as he watched her. Apparently the physical effects of Rapture lingered long after the regrets had settled in.

This was bad.

He'd mishandled everything.

Plus, he'd just had the best sex of his life. He pressed his lips together, threaded his fingers through his hair, tried to ignore the tenderness pushing against his heart.

*The drug. It's the drug.* He struggled to convince himself. It wasn't Elle. She was nothing special.

The minute the thought popped into his head, he knew it was a lie, an excuse. She *was* special. That was the problem.

She smoothed the skirt of her dress, ironing out wrinkles with the flat of her hand.

Fifteen minutes ago, his palms had been skimming over that luscious body of hers. But a lot could change in fifteen minutes.

She slipped her feet into her shoes and that's when Dante realized he was still naked, sitting up on the pool table, watching her get dressed, his dick as hard as steel between his legs.

Elle dropped her gaze and he saw that she'd noticed the condition he was in. She looked at his face again.

Tension radiated between them. It was almost as powerful as the passion they had just explored.

Dante gulped and tracked his eyes from her smoking-hot body to her face. The woman was a showstopper with those full, feminine hips, narrow waist and high, pert breasts. Her hair, which she normally wore pulled back or pinned up, tumbled about her shoulders in a riot of red curls. He'd nibbled off her lipstick during their lovemaking, but her mouth was slightly swollen and it had turned a deep, rosy pink from the pressure of their kisses.

Her expression was inscrutable, her gaze steady, eyes revealing nothing of what she might be feeling. He'd never met a woman who could tuck her real emotions away so surely.

Where had she learned that self-protective trick? Did it come naturally? Had she picked it up from her demanding job as a nurse? Or was it something living with Mark had taught her?

"Um," she said. "Thanks."

"Thanks?"

"You know." She lifted her shoulders in a shrug. "For the sexual release."

"You're welcome," he said, feeling awkward and stupid.

"It was…er…nice."

Nice? *Nice?*

His masculine ego took a helluva hit, because for him, it had been phenomenal. Then Dante realized she was covering her tracks, shoring up her defenses. She didn't want him to know how much it had affected her. She didn't trust him any more than he trusted her.

And rightly so.

"I'll see you around the hospital," she said.

"So this is it? A onetime thing." Why was he saying this? Of course it was a onetime thing. It couldn't be anything else.

"It's for the best."

She was dumping him? He was nothing more to her than a one-night stand? He felt like he'd been sucker punched, even though he'd been telling himself he had to make sure nothing like this happened again. He couldn't allow his sexual indiscretion to compromise the investigation.

"Sure," he said, making certain it came through in his voice that he didn't give a damn. "Whatever you want."

# 7

"ELLE? ARE YOU OUT HERE?"

The sound of Julie's voice echoing through the bottom part of the garage yanked Elle's attention away from the naked man on the pool table.

Their lovemaking had been brain-stunningly amazing.

No, not lovemaking, she corrected herself. Sex. Just scratch-an-itch sex. Nothing more.

What they'd had was raw and uninhibited sex and she'd loved it. She'd never had casual sex before and it felt a little weird but freeing. She wouldn't read anything into this encounter other than what it had been—two people coming together to give each other momentary pleasure.

No promises. No commitment. No strings attached. This was exactly what she needed.

"Elle? Where are you?"

"You better get dressed," she whispered to Dante. "It's my friends." Turning, she hurried toward the door leading down to the lower level, trying her best to ignore the alien feelings churning inside of her heart.

"Elle?" This time it was Vanessa.

"I'm on my way down," she called out, sending one last lingering look at Dante before she opened the door and plunged down the stairs.

The expression in his eyes was both sultry and dismissive. She could tell he wanted her, but he also wanted her gone.

Good. She felt the same way.

*Liar.*

She shoved that voice aside, forced a bright smile on her face as she spied her friends. "Hi, guys."

Julie and Vanessa stared at her.

Self-consciously, Elle raised a hand to her hair. "What?"

"Hmm," Vanessa observed with a tinkle in her eye. "Looks like somebody just got lucky."

"I don't know you mean," Elle said, not particularly anxious to come clean to her friends.

"Mused hair, swollen lips, cat-that-ate-the-canary grin. Please, I know a well-fucked look when I see it," Vanessa said.

Elle laughed because she didn't know what else to do. "Guilty as charged," she confessed.

"Honestly?" Julie looked shocked.

Elle couldn't help grinning. Her head was still pleasantly muzzy, her body warm and soft and wonderfully sated. The world looked kind and welcoming and loveable. "Um-hm."

"Who was it with?" Julie clasped her hands together. "Please don't tell me that it was Mark."

"Gag me!" Elle exclaimed. "Of course it wasn't with Mark. Why would you even think that?"

"Sometimes," Julie said, "when a girl is—"

"Horny," Vanessa finished for her.

Julie glowered. "I was going to say lonely. A girl will do things she normally wouldn't do."

"Like having mad sex with a near stranger on a pool table in Pete Russell's garage?" Elle supplied.

"A near stranger?" Vanessa asked, confusion marring

her expression. "So not a total stranger. It's someone you're acquainted with, but not well?"

"Anyone we know?" Julie asked. "Or is it a celebrity?"

"Shh." Vanessa winked and rested a finger against her lips. "We're from Confidential Rejuvenations. Your secret is safe with us."

Elle prayed Dante would keep quiet in the loft and not pick this moment to do something embarrassing like come strutting downstairs with his chest chuffed. "I don't kiss and tell."

She swished past her friends, eager to get out of the garage. She was still caught between feeling guilt and the lovely afterglow of phenomenal sex, and she didn't want to share either with her friends.

Selfish? Maybe. But she hadn't ever felt this sexually empowered and she wanted to keep this unexpected feeling all to herself.

A heated flush rose to her cheeks just thinking about what she had dared. She ducked her head and hurried toward the exit. Vaguely she heard Vanessa and Julie follow her past the Harleys, the Bentley, the Hummer and the Escalade and out the door into the late night breeze.

She checked her watch. Correction—an early-morning breeze. It well was after two on Saturday morning. She'd gone into the garage with Dante around midnight. Had they really made love for almost two hours? She'd been caught in such an exquisite time warp it had seemed like only minutes.

"Hey, wait up for us, why don't you?" Vanessa called out.

Why? Because she desperately needed to get away by herself, think things through and make some sense of what she was feeling.

"Well," Julie said as she and Vanessa caught up with her. "I for one think it's a good thing. You deserve a little happiness."

"It's not happiness. It was just sex," Elle said, trying to convince herself as much as her friends.

"Either way, it's smart to get back on the horse after you've been thrown." Vanessa nodded. "I think it is a good thing that it's just sex. You don't need any romantic complications. Not at this point in your life.

Vanessa was absolutely right. She was finally starting to get over Mark's betrayal, but she was far from emotionally ready to trust another man, especially one as darkly secretive as Dante Nash.

Elle stopped walking and hugged herself against the night air. She swayed, still feeling oddly loopy after her encounter with Dante. Smiling, she looked at Julie and Vanessa in the moonlight. "How did I get so lucky to have such great friends in my life?"

Julie laughed. "That's so like you, Elle. You're always there to pick up the pieces for us when we need you. It's our privilege to be there for you. Don't you know how wonderful you are?"

"Come on, chica." Vanessa was the one who had trouble expressing her more tender emotions. "I'll drive you home. You might have only had one cosmo, but the way you're swaying tells me you're too hopped up on the afterglow of great sex to be driving."

Elle didn't resist Vanessa's invitation. The truth was, the thought of sliding behind the wheel and having to concentrate on the road was daunting. Because no matter how hard she tried not to think about him, her mind kept slipping back to the pool table.

Back to Dante.

DANTE WOKE ON SATURDAY morning the day after Pete Russell's party with a pounding headache. *Rapture, my ass,* he thought. Lawson should have named the damned drug Fracture. That's how badly his head was hurting. Fracture would have gone over big with the Goth crowd.

And then he remembered Elle.

Guilt, vicious as a rabid dog, bit into him.

What in the hell was he going to do about Elle?

Before he had time to follow that train of thought, his cell phone rang. He sat up, one hand pressed flat against his aching temple, the other reaching for his cell phone on the nightstand. "Hello?"

"Nash, Briggins here."

"Yeah?" Dante squinted at the clock and was appalled to see it was after nine.

"What happened last night?"

"Huh?" For one panicky moment he thought Briggins was talking about what he'd done with Elle.

"What's your progress with Lawson?"

"He gave me a tablet of Rapture last night at Pete Russell's party."

"No shit?" Briggins said excitedly. "Bring it in and we'll get the lab to analyze it."

"I had to take it—it was a test. I had to prove to him that he could trust me. I think he's going to make me his business partner."

"Well done, Nash. Are you okay?"

"Fine."

"No adverse reactions?"

"Other than what feels like a hellish hangover."

"What was the drug like?" Briggins asked.

"Heightened sensory awareness. Heightened sexual desire and response. I can see why people take it."

"That good, huh?"

"The allure always has a dark side," Dante replied. "You're totally out of control. Basic instincts take over and you're operating on a primal level."

"You must have hated that," Briggins said. "You've got more self-control than most of us."

"It felt damned dangerous."

"Move forward cautiously. Remember, Gambezi is who we're really after. Lawson's small potatoes."

As if he could forget that—Leeza's death was forever burned in his brain. But Mark was the trail and Rapture was the breadcrumbs that led to Gambezi's door.

"I called because we've got another angle for you to follow."

"Oh?"

"We've just had an alert that one hundred thousand dollars in cash has been deposited into the checking accounting of Lawson's ex-wife."

"Excuse me?" His head was throbbing so badly, Dante thought he'd misunderstood.

"Looks to me like Elle Kingston might be on Gambezi's payroll. Either that or she's blackmailing her ex-husband and he paid her with the dirty money Gambezi paid him."

"Where is this assumption coming from?"

"The bills deposited into her account matched the serial numbers from an armored car heist last year in Houston that we suspect Gambezi's henchmen pulled off."

Dante drew in a harsh breath. He wanted to tell Briggins that it was impossible, that Elle simply could not be involved with Gambezi. She was too honest, open and aboveboard for that. He sure as hell didn't want to believe it. "You're certain?"

"I've got the computer printout of her bank statement right here."

"It seems fishy," Dante said. "Elle's no dummy. She's got to know large cash deposits are automatically reported to the IRS. Maybe she got the money from somewhere else."

"She's a middle-class nurse from a family of cops. Where's she going to get her hands on that kind of cash? And if it came through legitimate sources, there would be some kind of a paper trail."

"So what do you want from me?"

"Check it out. Find out where she got the money. Find out if she knows anything about Lawson's little hobby. If she's met Gambezi."

"Oh yeah, like that's going to slip nicely into a conversation."

"You'll find a way."

The notion bothered him. He didn't want to get any closer to Elle than he already was. "Why can't we do all this through Lawson?"

"We don't want Gambezi getting wind of this and going underground. The woman's safer than Lawson, but don't take any unnecessary chances."

Dante fisted his free hand. He thought of his mother, who'd abandoned him and his sister when they were just children. Thought of Leeza who'd turned to a gangster instead of her own brother when she'd gotten into trouble.

Somehow he'd failed her; he wouldn't fail Elle.

He shook his head. *You couldn't save them, no matter how much you loved them.* The pounding in his brain was severe and a nauseating knot had formed in his stomach. "I don't think this is such a good idea."

"What's the matter?" Briggins asked. "You're male,

she's female. Turn on your brooding-loner charm, women love that dark and tortured stuff."

"My charm isn't the issue, sir."

"No? Then go romance her and get her to spill all her secrets."

"It feels underhanded."

"No more underhanded than spying on Lawson."

"I don't want to hurt her."

"Nash, snap out of it and do your job."

Dante thought of how Elle had challenged him over Travis Russell. She was a good nurse. He simply could not believe she'd be involved with anything so harmful. He'd seen her with patients; Briggins had not. "We don't know for sure she's involved."

"We know she was married to Lawson and now there's one hundred thousand unexplained dollars in her checking account. Get over to her house, gain her trust and find out just where in the hell she got her hands on that kind of cash."

At the thought of seeing Elle again, Dante's spirits soared. Even without Briggins's orders, he'd been wanting to spend more time with her, needing to see her and make sure she was okay.

Now he had a perfect excuse and he couldn't get over to her house fast enough.

AT THE SAME TIME DANTE was talking to Briggins, Elle was waking up alone in her bed. Unlike her staff who pulled rotating days off, as head of the emergency department, Elle had her weekends free. She felt empty-headed and disoriented. What on earth had happened to her last night?

Her memory was fogged, but her lips were sore and her elbows skinned and the ache between her legs was something new. Then she glanced across the room at her rumpled green party dress flung carelessly over her vanity and it all came rushing back.

Dante.

The pool table.

Everything.

Her face flushed and she flopped back against the pillow, covering her eyes with her hands as each vivid detail filled her mind with startling clarity. The implications of her actions hit her full on and she groaned aloud.

How was she going to face Dante on Monday?

Dante Nash. Big and broad-shouldered and mysterious.

Her fingers tingled in memory of what it had felt like to touch his well-muscled body. What it tasted like to kiss his brooding lips. What his groans of pleasure had sounded like echoing in her ears.

A fresh shot of adrenaline whipped through her body and she gripped the sheet in her hands.

Last night, for the first time, she'd seen him away from the hospital and out of his expensively tailored suits or the standard-issue green scrubs. He'd looked crisp and fresh and collegiate in starched chinos and his white button-down shirt.

Preppy.

She wondered what his background was like. Where was he from? What did he do in his spare time? Who were his parents? Did he have any brothers or sisters?

But she had trouble imaging him being a regular person. Leading a regular life. He seemed so different than most of the men she'd known.

She wanted to know more about him, but curiosity was a dangerous thing. Last night had been great. Stupendous in fact, but there was no reason to go back to that well. She'd gotten what she needed—fabulous sex. Why not just accept the gift and let it go? It wasn't as if he had been panting to see her again.

Elle remembered the way Dante had looked at her afterward. As if he couldn't distance himself fast enough from what they'd done together. Okay, fine. She was a big girl. She could handle that.

While she was trying to convince herself, her phone rang. She propped herself up on the pillow, checked the caller ID and then reached for the receiver. "Hello, Char."

"Where are you?" Char asked.

"What do you mean where am I? It's Saturday morning and I had a late night of it. I'm in bed."

"You're supposed to be here. Everyone's asking where you are."

"Here?"

"You forgot about the family reunion? We're short an outfielder for the softball team and your mother wants to know if you're bringing the potato salad like you promised."

Elle groaned and immediately threw back the covers. Her feet hit the hardwood floor with a splat and she hurried to the bathroom with the cordless phone tucked against her chin. After her incredible sexual encounter with Dante, she had completely forgotten about the family reunion. "Char, tell everyone I'm so sorry and I'll be there as soon as I can."

"You forgot about the family reunion? How could you forget about the family reunion? I swear someone in your family calls me twice a day to remind me about it," Charlotte said.

"Look, some of us aren't as new to the family as you. We're not so enthused about the mandatory family reunion and the highly competitive softball tournament," Elle said, trying to brush her hair and talk on the phone at the same time.

"What happened last night?"

"Excuse me?" she asked as she dabbed on foundation.

"You said you had a late night of it. It must have been some night to make you forget about the family reunion and get so snippy."

Elle sighed. "I'm not being snippy—"

"Were you with Dante?" Char interrupted. "That would make me forget about a family reunion. Are you bringing him with you?"

"I'm not bringing Dante." Elle's voice rose.

"You don't have to get testy. I was only asking."

"Dante and I are not a couple." She smoothed blush on her cheeks. "Why would I bring him to a family reunion?"

"For fun?"

"He's not family." Using her index finger she blended eye shadow over her lids.

"Sorry I asked. So I'll tell your mother you're coming and you're bringing two gallons of mustard potato salad."

"Two gallons?" Her makeup finished, she hurried back to the bedroom, twisting out of her sleep shirt as she went.

"That's what she said. She thinks you're making it yourself so you better put it in your own container."

Elle groaned, pulled a pair of denim Capri pants from her drawer and shimmied into them.

At that moment the doorbell rang.

"Look, Char, someone's at the door." Fighting to hang on to the phone while she finished dressing, Elle put on a bra and then pulled a white baby-doll T-shirt over her head. "I gotta go, thanks for the heads-up and I'm sorry if I was snippy. I'll see you guys in about two hours."

"Two hours? Your dad's going to have a conniption. The first game will be over by then. Why two hours?"

"My car isn't here. I have to find someone to give me a ride to pick it up where I left it."

"You *did* have a wild night last night."

*You have no idea,* Elle thought.

"Hurry up," Charlotte admonished. "It's not the same without you."

Elle hung up, figuring it was probably Vanessa dropping by to give her a ride to Pete Russell's place to pick up her car. Quickly slipping on a pair of sneakers, she answered the door on the fourth chime of the bell.

But it wasn't Vanessa standing on her stoop. Rather it was the very man she'd been telling herself she needed to forget.

Dante was dressed much as she was. In jeans that perfectly encased his long legs and a snug-fitting T-shirt that showed off his biceps, running sneakers and a Texas Rangers baseball cap.

He cocked a loaded grin at her. "Hi."

"Hi," she said, unable to stop herself from smiling back.

"You ready?"

"Ready for what?"

"Your family reunion."

Elle narrowed her eyes. "Did Char call you?"

Dante shook his head. "No, but she invited me. You don't remember?"

What was going on here? Last night he had seemed cool and unaffected by what had transpired on the pool table, and now he was acting as if they were dating. Talk about mixed messages and mind games.

"I brought my bike," he said. "It's a nice day for a motorcycle ride, if you don't mind riding double."

"You have a bike?" She was a sucker for motorcycles and the men who rode them, while at the same time, as a nurse, she was well aware of the risks involved. Maybe that's what excited her.

The danger.

He jerked his head in the direction of the street and she peered over his shoulder to see a sleek, shiny red-and-black Ducati motorcycle parked at the curb.

"You're asking me out to my own family reunion?"

"You sound surprised." He leaned in closer.

"After last night—"

"This is to make up for last night."

"There's nothing to make up for," she said, shifting her weight from foot to foot. "Last night happened, it was great, and I have no expectations from you. You don't have to take me to my family reunion." It was true. She didn't have any expectations from him. Desires, yes, expectations, no.

"I was…" He hesitated. She could tell this was difficult for him by the way he self-consciously stuck his hands in his pockets and avoided her eyes. "Abrupt with you."

His awkward apology was touching and she couldn't resist the urge to rescue him. "Excuse me? Are you aware that we…um…made love for two hours? In my book that's not exactly abrupt."

"I meant afterward. I was abrupt with you afterward and that was wrong. I thought I might have made you feel…" His apology stalled again. Clearly he wasn't used to this. But then what doctor was accustomed to confessing a mistake? None that she had ever met.

"The only thing you made me feel was great, Dante. There's nothing to apologize for. We're good. You have my blessing to go on about your life."

For the first time since she'd known the man, he looked uncertain. "I was hoping," he said, "that we could be better than good."

Her heart scaled her throat. She wasn't ready for this. Didn't really want it. But the look in his eyes was doing very strange things to her stomach. "Meaning?"

"You're potato chips, Elle."

"Potato chips? Oh now that's what every girl wants to hear." If he didn't look so earnest, she would have laughed.

"What I mean is, with you, a guy has a hard time stopping with just one moment. Like you can't eat one potato chip."

"Potato chips are bad for you."

"True enough, but they taste so good."

She did laugh then. "I suppose I should be flattered."

"Okay, that sounded totally stupid," he agreed. "I'm out of practice with this sort of thing."

"What sort of thing? Asking out nurses?"

"Asking out anyone."

She sized him up. "I don't believe it. Guys like you have to swat women off like flies."

"Guys like me?"

"You know. Tall, dark, handsome and brooding."

"That's how you see me?"

"That's how you are," she said. "And the girls go ga-ga over that tortured-loner shtick."

"Do you?" He stepped across the threshold and into her living room.

It was all she could do to keep from taking a step back. She wasn't going to let him intimidate her. "Do I what?"

He lowered his voice. "Go ga-ga over tortured loners?"

She laughed. "I'm a nurse. I see enough torture in my job. I prefer sunny and well-adjusted."

"Is that why you married Mark?"

"Low blow."

"You're right," he admitted. "I never said women didn't ask me out. I said I was out of practice doing the asking." His cocky grin was back. "Now I'm doing the asking."

The sight of that smile caught Elle deep in the gut. He

smiled so infrequently that when he did she treasured it like gold. Involuntarily, she licked her lips. "How come you're out of practice asking women out?"

"Medicine is a demanding mistress."

"So you're a workaholic."

"Aren't most physicians?"

She crossed her arms over her chest. "I'm supposed to find workaholism appealing?"

"You're not making this easy for me."

"Why should I?"

"You're going to make me work for this second date." He took another step toward her. If he came any closer, the tips of their sneakers would be touching.

"Second date?" She raised her eyebrows and rubbed one foot against the back of her opposite heel. *Stay still. Don't let him know how much you want to cut and run.* "We never had a first date."

"What did we have?"

"A one-night stand."

"I prefer to call it a romantic liaison."

"What we had was much more elemental than any liaison," she said.

"True," he admitted. "But you stirred me in a way I haven't been stirred in a very long time. I want more."

"Potato chips again."

"Exactly."

"I'm not ready for any kind of a relationship. I've been divorced for only fourteen months."

He leaned in closer. She wanted to back up, get away from his distracting body heat, but she held her ground and met his gaze. "Did I say the word *relationship?*"

He had not.

"Come on," he said with a casual shrug and another

disarming grin that didn't seem to come naturally to such a complicated man, but she could see he was trying. "What's it going to hurt to spend one day playing softball with your family?"

"Obviously you don't know my family."

At that fortuitous moment her telephone rang again. It was probably her mother this time.

"If you'll excuse me, I need to get that." She inclined her head toward the door, a hint, using the phone call as her excuse to get rid of him before she did something totally stupid like take him by the hand, drag him into her bedroom and beg for a repeat performance of last night.

But Dante was having none of it. "Don't worry," he said. "I don't mind waiting on you."

*Crap, he wasn't leaving.*

She turned and went to the phone, and she heard Dante click her front door shut behind him. It was official. He was in her house now. Encroaching upon her territory. She didn't like it.

Elle picked up the phone, but she was so distracted by Dante's presence behind her, she didn't speak into the receiver. Her eyes kept running up and down the length of his long, masculine body. Without provocation, her mouth watered. She watched as he clasped his hands behind his back and walked over to study the figurines in her curio cabinet.

"Hello? Hello? Elle, you there?" Vanessa asked.

"Yes."

"Listen, I'm at Confidential Rejuvenations."

"What's up?"

"I got called in for a minor emergency surgery and it's turned into something of a three-ring circus."

Elle heard the tension in her friend's voice. "What is it? What's happened?"

"Something knocked out the transformer near the hospital and then the backup generator didn't come on, so we're a bit in the dark here."

"Do you need me to come in? I could be there in a couple of minutes."

"No, no, I just need the number of the company that services the generator. I thought you might have the info before I bothered Dr. Covey."

"Sure." Elle told her where to find the information. "You're certain you don't need me?" Having to go to work would be the perfect excuse for missing the family picnic and softball tournament.

"It's really not a big thing. Mostly I'm handling patient grumbling. You know how it is when bigwigs don't get their way."

"I'm coming over."

"No, no," Vanessa said. "Enjoy your day off."

"Okay, all right. And thanks for letting me know. Don't hesitate to call if you need me."

"Gotta go. I'll give you all the details later. Have fun."

Elle hung up to find Dante standing too near, crowding her space.

"I've got a ride waiting at the curb," he said. "Ready to take you wherever you need to go."

"I have to go to Pete Russell's to pick up my car," she said. "Then I have to go to the grocery store, pick up two gallons of potato salad, come back here, put it in one of my containers so my mother won't know I didn't make it myself and get over to Lady Bird Park in an hour."

"You'll never make it."

"Tell me."

"How about this," he said. "We leave your car at Pete

Russell's for now. I make the potato salad and we cruise on over to the park with minutes to spare."

"You know how to make potato salad?"

"I have talents you know nothing about," he said slyly.

She narrowed her eyes. "Where did you learn how to make potato salad?"

"Kitchen duty in the army."

"You were in the army."

"Two years. That's how I paid for college."

"No kidding."

He shrugged.

"So you weren't always Dr. Armani with Gucci shoes and a Rolex?"

"Not by a long shot." He rubbed his palms together. "Now the big question—do you have enough potatoes to make two gallons of potato salad?"

"No," she admitted, "but I've got a next door neighbor who loves to cook. I'll pop over and see if she's got some spuds I could borrow. Seriously, you can make potato salad?"

"Seriously," he said washing his hands at her kitchen sink. "And I can make it in about thirty minutes. Now, go see about those potatoes."

# 8

FIVE MINUTES LATER they were standing side by side at Elle's sink, peeling russet potatoes. On the stove, eggs came to a boil, steaming up her cozy kitchen in a way it hadn't been steamed up in years. When she was married to Mark, he loved going out to eat, and since Elle was only a passable cook, she hadn't minded.

But now, watching Dante's thick, long fingers work the potato peeler with accomplished ease, she was beginning to understand how food could be very erotic.

A man who could cook—was there anything sexier?

From the corner of her eye, she watched him swiftly dice a potato on the cutting board and dump the slices into her big stainless-steel pot. She loved the way the muscles in her forearms bunched and the easy way he handled a knife.

But of course he would know how to use a blade—he was a surgeon. His job required precision, skill, nerves of steel.

Never in her life had she been so acutely aware of anyone. Of his elbow resting so close to hers, of his upper arm almost touching her shoulder, of his body heat, his overt masculinity.

Elle reached for the faucet to rinse off a potato at the very moment Dante did the same.

Their fingers bumped and she felt a wildfire of sensation spread throughout her nerve endings. Elle caught her breath and darted a glance in his direction.

His head was cocked to one side and he was staring at her with sultry, heavy-lidded eyes. Although he pressed his lips tightly together, she could see what he was trying to hide.

Stark, hungry need.

His eyes met hers and the air between them seemed to hold the promise of something so compelling she could not tear her gaze from his face.

There was no denying it. Both of them were breathing more quickly, and when he slowly reached out to brush a loose strand of hair from her forehead, Elle just froze.

Dante canted his head and studied her.

"What?" She reached up to touch the cheek he'd just singed with his fingers.

"I was thinking how beautiful you are," Dante said.

"What's going on?" she said, taking a step away from him, searching for some space. "What's with the full-court press?"

"What do you mean?"

"Last night, after we…um…"

"Made love," he said.

"Had sex," she replied firmly. "You were all, like, oops, big mistake. And then you show up on my doorstep and now you're making potato salad for my family. What happened overnight?"

He shrugged. "Change of heart."

"Well, I didn't. Last night was better than great, but, Dante, I don't want a relationship with you."

"I don't think I asked you for one."

"So what do you want?"

He looked at her for so long without speaking she'd about given up on the idea of having her question answered when he said, "I suppose I'm trying to figure you out."

"Huh?" She hadn't expected him to say that.

"You're a bit of an enigma, and that intrigues me," he said.

*I'm the enigma,* she thought. *Talk about the pot calling the kettle black.*

Elle had never been called an enigma before. If anything, she considered herself an open book. Sure, she had developed a talent for keeping her emotions under wraps since it was not only part of her job description as head nurse, but a skill she'd honed growing up in a family of cops.

"I'm afraid you're barking up the wrong girl. I'm not that interesting." She dropped her gaze and concentrated on peeling the potato.

"Oh," he said, a smug smile curling up his lips. "I beg to differ. Last night you—"

"Last night was very out of character for me," she interrupted. "I don't act like that."

"What was so different about last night?"

*You,* she wanted to say but didn't. "I wasn't feeling quite like myself."

Dante leaned forward, his head turned, eyes intent on her face. "What did you feel like?"

"Loose, relaxed, as if I wasn't even in my own skin." Thinking back on it, she had been feeling very odd and it was difficult to articulate what she'd felt.

"Anything else?"

The way he was looking at her made her think about the way her father used to interrogate her when she dared to break curfew, which hadn't happened but once or twice. One grilling by Tom Kingston Sr. was more than enough for any teenaged girl. It was unsettling and she was tempted not to answer Dante, but she found herself saying, "I had a cosmo. It tasted weird so I didn't drink all of it, but—"

A frantic hissing sound erupted from the stove, interrupting her.

"Oops, oops, the egg water is boiling over," she said, tearing her gaze from his and diving for the stove.

In her rush, Elle lost her balance and Dante thrust out an arm to catch her before she fell. He snapped the fire off underneath the eggs with one hand, while wrapping the other arm around her waist.

The man had amazing reflexes.

Her breasts skimmed his biceps. Her cotton V-neck T had risen up in the process and his hand flattened against her bare belly.

It felt as if everything was moving in slow motion as he pulled her back to her feet.

"Whoa there," he said, his mouth dangerously close to her ear.

Her stomach rippled. Her nipples hardened. She didn't want this reaction—or hell, maybe she did. The pleasure of his touch was undeniable. Maybe he was a potato chip, too—you couldn't be satisfied with just one.

After what seemed an eternity but was in reality mere seconds, he let go of her belly to slide his palm around to the small of her back and turned her to face him.

She wished he would stop touching her.

Or maybe she was kidding herself because all at once she was leaning against him for support, her eyes glued on his lips. The very same intoxicating lips that had driven her crazy with desire the night before.

This was completely nuts. There was nothing erotic about standing in her kitchen making potato salad.

But she wanted him to kiss her again.

His head was lowered and his hand was at her back and she was looking up at him—waiting.

Her eyes shuttered closed as she thought about the pressure of his lips on hers, hungering for the sensation that had so captivated her in Pete Russell's pool room.

Insanity.

*Stop this, Elle.*

Okay, it might be insane, but the truth of it was she liked his touch, ached to feel his arms around her again, and yearned to have his mouth back on hers. She wanted him to hold her and kiss her and never let her go.

"Elle?"

She opened her eyes, breaking the mental trap she'd fallen into. He met her gaze. "Yes?"

"Are you okay?"

"Fine, great, never better."

"You had a funny look on your face."

"Did I?" she said faintly.

"You did," he confirmed.

"I was thinking about Vanessa and what's going on over at the hospital."

"I think you're a liar." He shifted closer and the movement spiked her pulse. "But a very sexy one."

His lips were mere inches away and getting closer with each erratic strum of her heart.

He was staring so hard at her mouth and the blood was pumping through her veins and his hand was hot against her skin. His eyes narrowed in a sexy, somnolent expression that she couldn't resist edging the tiniest bit closer to him.

"I think you were thinking about this," he murmured, and then he gave her what she'd been yearning for.

The full brunt of his lips.

Dante's mouth tasted like golden, star-dusted honey and she instantly forgot everything else. He branded her with his fevered tongue, blistering her with the heat of his rising passion.

Elle's heart plunged, tripping her pulse in a frantic rhythm of stimulus and response. Dreamily, she sighed against his mouth. She'd been craving this all morning and she hadn't even realized it until now.

A scorching heat flashed through her, incinerating everything in its path—her tongue, her throat, her chest and beyond. She burned from the glorious pressure of his lips.

Burned for him.

No one else's kiss had ever affected her like this. Certainly not Mark's, not even in the early days. This craving Dante stirred in her was new and different and scary as hell.

Dante's kiss took her breath, took her brain, took every ounce of resistance she possessed.

The scrape of his beard stubble against her tender skin only added to the erotic sensations he stirred inside her. Naked need erupted from him into her and spun a silken web of magic that went far beyond the mere joining of their lips.

She was ready to throw in the towel on her self-control and push him to the bedroom, and then Dante pulled away.

"To be continued," he murmured. "We've got to get these potatoes on to boil if we're going to make it to the park by your one-hour deadline."

Forty minutes later, the potato salad was made, packaged in Tupperware and Dante had already washed up the pans, cutting board and utensils he'd used.

"That is awesome potato salad. My mother is going to be so jealous," Elle said after she'd spooned a bite of it into her mouth. "Who knew that you were so much more than a pretty face? He cooks, he cleans, he operates. I still can't figure out why you're single."

He didn't comment, just put the potato salad in the plastic bag she'd got out of the pantry for him. "Let's roll," he said, reached for her hand and led her to the door.

His palm was warm and his grip firm. Holding hands with him felt way too intimate. Holding hands was something sweethearts did and they definitely were not sweethearts. She tried discreetly to pull her hand from his, but he stubbornly held on tight. Her stomach did that strange loopy thing, and she felt at once both panicked and disarmed.

He took an extra helmet from his motorcycle saddlebags and stowed the potato salad in the spot where the helmet had been.

"Here you go," he said and settled the helmet on her head. She pulled it down tight and then he reached over to click the snap closed beneath her chin.

He swung one leg over the bike, got it started and then held his hand out to help her astride. She sank down onto the thick leather seat behind him, her heart strumming.

Once she was set, he took off. Elle let out an involuntary squeal of delight. He zoomed through traffic, headed for Lady Bird Park, which was only a few miles from Elle's house.

Beneath her clasped hands, she could feel Dante's six-pack abs rippling when he moved. They took a hairpin curve at a clip that had her holding her breath and tightening her grip around his waist.

"You did that on purpose." She raised her voice to be heard above the engine noise,

He turned his head toward her, flashed her a grin. "Prove it."

Her inner thighs were wrapped around his outer thighs,

his hard muscles sweetly rigid underneath her soft ones. Her crotch settled flush against his firm butt. She felt all warm and melty inside.

To distract herself from sexy thoughts, Elle stared out across the grassy freeway embankments, which were awash in a sea of bluebonnets and Indian paintbrushes, as they usually were this time of year in the Texas Hill Country. The wind was cool on her face. The smell of spring hung rich and earthy on the air.

As they neared the exit ramp to the park, Dante slowed the motorcycle and switched on his turn signal.

The look on her family's face when they came zooming into the picnic area was priceless.

Her two older brothers, Phillip and Ben, decked out in their softball jerseys, dropped their jaws when they saw Dante's motorcycle and realized their baby sister was riding on the back.

The park was full of Kingstons who'd taken over five picnic areas—her parents, siblings, uncles, aunts, cousins, nieces and nephews, three-quarters of them cops. The men in the bunch converged on them, looking as if they had chips on their shoulders and were aching for Dante to knock it off.

Without even thinking, Elle slipped her arm through Dante's and then immediately wondered why she'd done so. She glanced around at her family, who'd been there for her when Mark had dumped her. They were a loving bunch who always gave her a soft place to land when she fell, and she knew they were only worried about her.

She took a deep breath and put a big smile on her face. "Family, this is Dr. Dante Nash. Dante, the family."

GETTING FRIENDLY WITH Elle was much easier than Dante had thought it was going to be, especially after their awkwardness the night before at Pete Russell's house. The woman trusted too easily. She'd let down her guard, let him right into her house, even as she protested their relationship wasn't a relationship.

Dante knew better. She wanted more—he wanted more, too—and here he was taking advantage of her desires. She excited him as no woman ever had, and that was a scary thing.

But this was the hard part. Getting friendly with her family.

He'd never been good with other people's families, probably because he'd never been good with his own. There was only him and his father left now, and he hadn't seen his old man in fifteen years. It was his dad's choice, not his.

He was an instant hit with Tina, Elle's mother. The homemade potato salad went a long way in claiming her affections. And to be honest, he really liked the older woman. She was the epitome of the mom he'd never had. Watching her lovingly tend her brood caused something in the center of his chest to shift oddly.

"A man who cooks?" she said, after Elle explained he'd made the side dish. "Don't let this one get away, daughter."

Dante's eyes met Elle's.

Pink splotches of embarrassment stained her cheeks. Her reaction, along with the unexpected rush of tenderness that assailed him, surprised him.

Her sisters-in-law and female cousins had his attention as they gathered around, asking him about being a surgeon to celebrities. But Elle's father, brothers, uncles and male cousins were a different matter all together.

If these men knew what he had done to Elle last night, he had no doubt they would clobber him within an inch of his life. They were cops, officers of the law, and as such, they had a strong sense of justice but with a potent protective streak.

Dante didn't take offense—he understood. He had been equally protective of Leeza.

Glancing around the park, at the picnic tables laden with food, he experienced a sudden, inexplicable sense of loss and alienation. He didn't belong here, and yet a yearning for this kind of connection to family that he'd never had and had never admitted to wanting tightened his throat.

The delicious smell of mesquite-grilled hamburgers and bratwurst filled the air. Elle's mother set his potato salad down to join containers of cole slaw, spicy baked beans, corn on the cob and broccoli casserole. Dessert was a bountiful selection of melons, chocolate cake and peanut butter cookies. Three two-gallon ice-cream freezers churned with homemade banana ice cream. There was punch for the kids, sun tea for the adults and iced beer for those in the mood.

Elle, Dante noticed, was in rare form. Playing with the children, laughing at her brothers, girl-talking with her mother, sisters-in-law, aunts and cousins. At work, she was all business, sharp and quick and smart. But here, among her family, he saw just how open and fun loving she could be.

The meal was incredible, the company even more so. And when lunch was over, the conversation turned to the softball tournament.

Not long afterward, Dante found himself wearing a Kingston family jersey and squatting behind home plate in a catcher's mask. He watched the Kingston clan gleefully gear up to smack the softball around.

He and Elle ended up on opposing teams and her team went first. When it was Elle's turn at bat, Dante was confronted by a very appealing view.

No matter how hard he tried not to ogle her in front of her father and brothers, he couldn't stop his gaze from straying over her body. She stood at home plate, her tight little Capri pants clinging provocatively to her hips and thighs as she wiggled her butt, swishing the bat through the air in a couple of warm-up swings. The way her T-shirt molded to her chest made Dante's mouth run dry. The V-neck scooped low, revealing a spectacular pair of tits. High and round. Not too big, not too small, just right.

Then, for absolutely no reason at all, he stopped abruptly, almost overcome by what he was feeling. Why? What was this all about?

From early childhood, he'd been taught to swallow back his emotions and ignore them in favor of cool-headed logic. Growing up abandoned by his mother and knocked around by his father, Dante had learned to fight, to protect what was his and that the only two feelings a man could rely on were vengeance and anger. The rest led him to places that hurt too damned much.

But suddenly, here he was, feeling a simple yearning that resonated all the way into his bones. A yearning born of years of denying the things he really wanted but never thought he could have.

A home. A family. Love.

It was a dangerous dream.

The idea of it sliced him up inside.

His gaze tracked back to Elle, who'd got a hit and was running toward first base. Her auburn curls were flying in the breeze, her breasts bouncing prettily as she ran against the backdrop of a bright blue spring sky, red dirt and green grass. Yellow rays of sunlight splashed her body and he imagined a beatific smile lit up her face.

His heart twisted.

A single glance at her and the power of their chemistry vibrated through him like an electrical pulse. He felt it in his lungs, in his throat, tight around his ankles like shackles, light as a drawn breath, thick as blood.

She must have sensed that his gaze was upon her because when she made it safely to first base, she tossed her head and turned to stare at him.

Dante squeezed his eyes shut and in that pop of difference between the bright noonday sun and the darkness behind his eyelids, he experienced the oddest sensation of falling down a long, black, empty tunnel.

His eyes flew open and he shifted his attention to the pitcher. Elle's brother Phillip was up to bat.

"You hurt my sister and my brothers and I will cut your balls off," Phillip said cheerfully.

"What?" Dante asked, startled by the comment.

"I've seen the way she looks at you. She's vulnerable, on the rebound. Elle's been through enough with that bastard Mark. She doesn't need you screwing her over."

"I'm not going to hurt her."

"That's good. Because that thing I said about cutting off your balls? I meant it," Phillip said, then promptly smacked the softball far into left field.

Dante had no doubt that he did.

As he watched Elle round the bases to third with her older brother hot on her heels, he couldn't help wishing that he hadn't just told a big fat lie. No matter how you sliced it, he *was* going to hurt Elle.

The guilt Dante had been feeling was back, vicious as ever.

Elle was running for home, legs churning in the red sand, auburn curls tumbling about her face. The outfield hurled the ball toward home plate. The Kingston clan who were standing on the sidelines were screaming excitedly.

"Come on, Elle, come on, come on, come on."

"Tag her out, Dante."

"You can do it!"

"Get her, get her."

Elle's eyes were on his; Dante's were on hers, not on the ball where they should be. But then again, her eyes weren't on home plate, either. Her gaze was on him, fully, completely, and the look was undeniably hungry.

She barreled straight toward him.

In the dugout, her team was jumping up and down, waving their baseball caps and cheering.

His team was rushing forward.

The softball seemed to hang in the sky in what seemed like a slow-motion free fall. Everyone held their collective breaths.

Finally, Dante tore his gaze off Elle and redirected his glove at the ball.

Elle dove, sliding into home plate, red dust flying in the air…just as Dante jumped up and snagged the ball in a midair catch.

"Safe," screamed Elle's team.

"She's out," hollered Dante's.

"His feet were off the base when he caught it!"

"You're wrong."

Both teams flooded the field, converging on home plate like a swarm of ants. They were all arguing and shouting at once, no one paying the least bit of attention to anyone else, all of them caught up in the excitement and controversy.

Elle was on her back on the ground looking up at him.

Dante loomed over her, the softball clutched tightly in his glove.

Their gazes wed. Neither one of them could look

away. She smiled at him so sweetly that Dante had to smile back.

"I warned you," she said. "My family is very passionate about their softball. You sure you want to get mixed up with a bunch like this?"

Before he could answer, Elle's father clamped him on the shoulders. "So tell us, Dante, from your point of view, is Ellie in? Or is she out?"

# 9

DANTE REACHED A HAND down to help Elle up, his big, masculine fingers encircling her wrist. He tugged her to her feet, and then leaned over to brush dirt from the seat of her pants.

The gesture was overly familiar and not at all like something he would normally do, and it lit a fire deep within Elle. She stood before him, unable to look at anything else but him, ignoring the sounds of her family squabbling over the game and the fact that her father was standing right behind Dante.

"I was out," she said softly, her gaze hooked on Dante's lips.

"You were safe," he insisted.

"You caught the ball as I slid into home plate. Clearly, I was out."

"I had both feet off the bag when I caught the ball, you were solidly safe."

"What's with you two?" Phillip asked. "Elle shouldn't be saying she was out and you shouldn't be saying she was in."

"Does it really matter?" Elle asked.

"Does it matter?" about ten members of her family exclaimed in unison. "Of course it matters!"

And then they were off talking about family tradition and competitive sportsmanship and softball as a metaphor for life.

"Does your family ever act like this?" Elle asked with a grin.

"I don't have a family," he said.

That took her aback and it struck her how very little she knew about him. "No one?"

"Not anymore."

"Mother? Father? Siblings?

"All gone."

She wanted to ask him what happened, but the look in his eyes warned her off. That and the family coming to an agreement that Elle had officially been safe. Taking the victory she didn't care about in the least, she went to sit in the dugout beside Charlotte and her mother while Dante returned to home plate in his position as catcher.

As the game progressed and the sun grew hotter, some of the men started taking off their shirts. The ladies in the stands and in the dugout and on the field issued catcalls. By and large the Kingston men were in very good physical shape and the Kingston women appreciated their men.

"Woo-hoo, take it off, Tom," Charlotte hollered at her husband.

"Let's see it, babe." Elle's mother called to her father. "Show the kids that they aren't the only ones who've got the goods."

Elle's father good-naturedly stripped off his shirt, revealing that even at fifty-six he was still a toned, athletic man. She had to admit that her family had been blessed with good genes.

The game came to a standstill as it turned into an all-out striptease, with the men strutting their stuff and flinging shirts about the softball diamond, until Dante was the only male still wearing his.

"Dante, Dante, Dante." One of Elle's female cousins started a slow chant and clapped her hands.

The others picked it up and soon every woman on their side of the park was chanting, "Dante, Dante, Dante."

Elle knew he was not used to this kind of familial ribbing. She wouldn't have blamed him if he'd bolted for the Ducati, took off and never spoke to her again. The Kingstons could come on pretty strong, but then again, he was the one who'd shown up at her door insisting on bringing her here.

Then Dante surprised her.

"You wanna see some of this?" he asked the crowd and pointed at his chest with both thumbs. This wasn't the serious, brooding doctor she knew. Curious, Elle leaned forward in her seat.

More catcalls ensued as Dante slowly began pulling his shirt over his head. Charlotte brought two fingers to her mouth and let loose with a long whistle so loud that Tom, who was on the field at shortstop, scowled at his new bride.

"Charlotte!" Elle exclaimed.

"Hey." Charlotte shrugged. "Just 'cause I'm on a diet doesn't mean I can't read the menu. Besides, I'm doing this for you."

"For me?"

"Getting him out of his clothes so you can have a view of what you're missing by not hooking up with him."

If only Charlotte knew.

Dante wrestled off the shirt and twirled it over his head like a Chippendale dancer. Giggling, Elle blushed and covered her eyes with her hand.

"We're not shy," a couple of Elle's elderly aunts said as they threw dollar bills onto the softball field. The entire group hooted with laughter.

Elle peeped at Dante's bare chest. Last night in Pete Russell's garage, she'd been too swept away by her hormones to fully appreciate what a buff stud Dante really was. Every muscle in his chest was ripped, rock-hard and clearly defined. He had the best body of any man on the softball diamond and that was saying a lot amidst a park full of well-chiseled men.

The only thing she hadn't counted on was the twinge of jealousy clawing through her as the other women ogled her man.

*Her man?*

Where had that thought come from? Immediately she batted it away.

The game continued for another hour, the field loaded with half-naked men. They took a break before the next game, after Dante's team won six to five when he hit a home run in the final inning.

Everyone came back to the picnic area for another round of food and drink. Elle saw her brothers drag Dante over to the ice chests and proceed to pour a beer over his head, crowning their reigning champion with suds. Elle was sitting under an elm tree drinking sun tea and nibbling one of her mother's homemade brownies when her father came over to perch on the picnic bench beside her.

"So, Dad," she said. "What do you think about Dante?" Her father had been the only one in her family who had seen through Mark and pegged him for the feckless jerk he was; she trusted his judgment.

"I like him." Her father nodded. "He's smart and observant and a damned fine athlete. But you should be careful where Dante Nash is concerned."

Her heart rate kicked up at her father's words of caution. "Why's that?"

"Because I'm fairly certain the man is hiding something."

"What do you mean?"

"I don't know what it is, but I've been a cop long enough to know someone with a big secret when I see him, and I'm afraid if you let your feelings for this guy get out of hand, you're going to get hurt again."

"I'm a big girl, Dad."

He leaned over to tousle her hair. "That's true but a father can't help how he feels about his daughter. You'll always be my little girl. You take people at face value, kitten, and you love too hard. Not everyone is worthy of your loyalty and trust."

"I can't help it."

"I know." Her father sighed. "You're like your mother. And where would I have been if she hadn't seen through my macho bluster and male bravado and fallen in love with me in spite of it? I wouldn't have all this." He swept his hand at the gathered family and a nostalgic smile tilted his lips. "And I wouldn't have you." With the crook of his arm, he pulled her against him and kissed the top of her head. "Remember, no matter what happens, we're here for you."

Elle's chest tightened with love for her father. "Thanks, Daddy."

He smiled and stood up from the table. "I'm going after a beer. You want one?"

She shook her head. She knew then that the vast affection of her family was what allowed her trust so easily and love so hard. They were her safety net.

She thought of Dante and all that he missed by not having a loving family, and sadness crowded her heart. The need to take him in and nurture him was overwhelming, but she couldn't take a grown man in as if he were some helpless fawn she'd found in the forest.

She took another look at him standing off to one side,

toweling the beer from his hair with his T-shirt, an unreadable expression on his face, his body language tight and aloof. This man was anything but helpless and she must resist the urge to take care of him.

While they'd been playing softball, a dark cloud had blown in, cooling off the day and the wind picked up. A gust snatched a batch of paper napkins from the table and scattered them across the grass. Elle went to pick them up.

The first drops of rain spattered the ground with fat wet plops. Within minutes the rain was coming down in sheets, sending everyone grabbing supplies and scurrying for the cars. From the looks of the black clouds bunching in the sky, the outdoor party was over.

She knew most of her family would motor on over to her parents' house to play cards or charades or dominoes and spend the evening munching on leftovers. Normally she would have gone with them.

But today wasn't normal.

Today her car was still parked at Pete Russell's house.

Today she was with Dante.

Today Elle was different in a way she did not understand.

Dante was at his motorcycle, starting it up, still barechested, his beer soaked T-shirt fed through his belt loop. "You should go with your family," he said. "Get in out of the rain."

She should. It's what a sensible person would do. It's what she would normally do. But something inside of her didn't feel sensible or normal. Stupid as it might seem, she wanted to take a risk, take a gamble, live a little.

"I'm coming with you," she said breathlessly, recklessly. It felt right. She threw a leg over the side of the bike, jammed the helmet down over her head as a rush of wind blew water from the leaves of the trees onto their shoulders.

The slightest of grins lit up Dante's eyes, but his mouth barely moved. He said nothing, just took her hands and latched them around his bare waist. Once he was sure she was secure, he took off.

A laugh exploded unexpected from her lungs, the sensation of pure joy taking her utterly by surprise.

And she'd thought the ride to the park had been thrilling!

Nothing had prepared her for this. Riding through the rain, the warm engine vibrating up through the leather seat, her hands clutched against his naked abdomen slick with rain. It was the ultimate turn-on.

Lightning flashed, sending a vivid fork of electricity through the cloud-filled sky. Thunder rumbled. Her heart was a racehorse galloping free across an open range. She relished being hooked up with this man. Elle couldn't ever remember feeling so alive.

Her nipples beaded hard. She tightened her grip around him, rested her head against his back, absorbing his body heat, reveling in the contact.

By the time they reached her house, they were drenched. She told Dante to park his bike under her carport and they ran laughing into the house.

When the door closed behind them, they turned to look at each other as they dripped soggily on the tile floor, and every thought went right out of Elle's head except one: *I have to have this man now.*

Dante must have had the identical thought because he moved toward her at the same moment she moved toward him.

He pulled her to his chest.

She flung her arms around his neck.

The pulse at the hollow of his throat was jumping.

Her heart was slamming against her rib cage.

His lips came down on hers.

She inhaled him, cupping both hands against the back of his head as hormones sent a rage of lust rushing through her blood.

He broke the kiss just long enough to murmur her name and press her back against the refrigerator. His tongue flickered crazily across her lips.

Immediately her body softened involuntarily in his arms and her teeth parted, letting him in.

Their lips fit so perfectly together, snug as the right lid for the right pot, that Elle stopped trembling. She kept her eyes open because she wanted to see his face. His eyes were open, too. He was watching her intently, gauging her reaction, trying to figure what she was feeling. That alone was wildly arousing.

Elle ached for him. Sure, she'd been around the block a time or two and she was over thirty years old, been married and divorced. She'd had a few lovers.

But this kiss… It was ten times better than the one the night before and that had been pretty darn legendary.

This was raw and hungry. Possessive. It was ominous and demanding.

Naked need, passionate frustration, pure animal lust erupted from him into her and spun a magic web that went far beyond the mere joining of their lips. This single, wild union was everything.

Everything.

Dante fisted his hand tighter in her hair and pulled her even closer to him, penetrating her with his tongue, exploring her fully.

She stopped thinking, stopped listening to her mental chattering. She stopped doing anything except allowing the moment to unfold. He was all that she'd ever envisioned in a lover and so much more. Tender yet decisive, and slow yet direct.

He groaned low in his throat. His body strained and pushed against hers and Elle met him measure for measure, cupping his face in her palms, marveling at the feel of his thick, warm skin.

His lips vibrated against hers and he breathed her name. "Elle."

She moaned quietly and he swallowed up the resonant hum of her.

Her emotions flailed giddily. Excitement warred with guilt and passion and sadness and glee. She wanted to laugh. She wanted to cry. She wanted to run.

She could feel the powerful muscles of his forearm tense against the back of her neck as he splayed his fingers through the damp strands to drape them over her shoulders.

He looked at her and his irises darkened with pleasure. Elle stared back, but unable to bear the tension, she looked away.

His touch was uncomplicated but compelling.

Furtively, she glanced at Dante. He was still staring at her. Incredulous.

She felt a little incredulous herself. There was no mistaking the spark of sexual attraction on his face. Desire shadowed the hollows of his cheeks, giving him a lean and dangerous look.

His eyes lowered in a heavy-lidded, totally masculine ogle. He wet his lips. Dante seemed quite turned on by the fact they were soaking wet in her kitchen.

Elle held that indrawn breath, waiting, hoping, afraid to exhale. She could smell the rain on his skin and she wondered how many women before her had been this close to him. A lot, she was certain.

But none of them, she decided, had ever really gotten to know him. She could feel it in him. A sixth sense. An instinct.

Did she dare go there?

His gaze was inscrutable, giving nothing away, but he was combing his fingers through her hair, lulling her, drawing her back under his spell.

She had to find a way to distract him. If he kept touching her like that she was going to get naked with him, and as much as she wanted him, she was afraid to go there again.

She wasn't the only one totally blown away. Eddies of embarrassment and sexual hunger washed over her, warring with waves of boldness and timidity.

"Dante…"

What was she going to say? She reached out, not knowing what she intended to do, but getting caught up in the crazy push-pull battling inside her, yearning to touch his cheek.

Dante raised an arm, blocking her hand, and latched his gaze onto hers. He was breathing hard and he did not speak. He didn't have to speak. She could read the message in his eyes loud and clear.

*I want to take you to bed.*

The resulting thrill that raced through her body was so powerful she almost had an orgasm right there on the spot.

*If you go to bed with him now, it's no longer a one-night stand. It'll be a relationship. He's starting to mean something to you.*

There it was. The thought they'd both been toying with in their heads for weeks. Wanting yet avoiding out of fear and uncertainty.

She knew all the rational reasons why it was wrong. Why the relationship was doomed to fail. She was on the rebound from Mark. Dante was a secretive guy who didn't know how to share his feelings. They were coworkers. He was Mark's friend. They were all sensible arguments, but sometimes you had to take a leap of faith and follow your heart.

*And if you get hurt?*

Screw it. If she got hurt, she got hurt. She flung her arms around his neck and kissed him again.

DANTE STOPPED KISSING her and drew back to look at Elle. He whispered her name. He felt scared all the way to his toes.

He didn't want to stop kissing her, but he couldn't think rationally when his lips were on hers. The desire she stirred in him was at odds with his sworn duty. He'd always had a strong moral compass. A certain sense of right and wrong. But being undercover, being unsure of where he stood, of having to do things that went against his ethical code had placed him squarely at the center of an ambiguous crossroads.

His assignment was to get close to her and gain her trust, but he couldn't help feeling guilty and underhanded, especially now that he was growing more and more certain she did not know anything about Mark's operation.

Her wide-eyed vulnerability cut him to ribbons. All he wanted was to take her into his arms and tell her everything was going to be okay. He knew it was a dangerous impulse, stupid even, but there it was. His infernal need to rescue her.

Dante's gaze drifted lazily down along her chin to the hollow of her throat to her chest where he could see her nipples pebbled against her bra beneath her thin, wet cotton T-shirt.

That's when he forgot about all the reasons why he could not make love to Elle again.

He held the rainstorm responsible for what happened next—it was too damned erotic. This was precisely why he didn't normally do things like take beautiful women for rides on his bike during a spring shower. He'd held back his desires for so long, tamped down his passion, ignored his libido. But once let loose, his hormones could not be herded back inside where they belonged.

The rain wasn't wholly at fault, though. He also blamed the softball game and her loving family and the hot noonday sun that had caused him to take off his shirt in a daring striptease. He also held accountable the sweet tilt of Elle's supple mouth and the seductive gleam in her delightful blue eyes, daring him, just daring him to do something naughty.

Most of all, he blamed himself. He should never have put either of them in this position.

She held out a hand to him and waited expectantly. He was trying to decide if he should go through with this or call Briggins up and insist he be taken off the case before he got in too deep.

Too late.

Elle zapped him with a meaningful stare and he felt as though he'd taken a stun gun jolt straight to his heart.

*Take that and that and that,* her blue eyes said.

She so stripped him to his soul and the next thing Dante knew, they were ripping off their clothes and stumbling for her bedroom, kissing and touching and stroking along the way.

"This is a very dumb thing to do," he murmured against her lips, needing to say the words even though he knew it was too late for either of them to stop. This moment had been a long time building. They'd crossed an invisible threshold and retreat was impossible.

"Sometimes being dumb is the smartest thing you can be," she said.

That totally made no sense, but at this point, he pretended her words were pearls of rare wisdom. They could worry about the consequences later, when their judgment wasn't glazed with the bright sheen of lust.

And then they were in her bedroom, kicking aside the covers, crawling wet and shivering into the dry sheets. They were both totally naked and he wasn't sure how they'd gotten that way or how he would survive what was going to happen next.

"You sure you want to do this?" he panted, breaking their kiss. The last thing he wanted was for her to have regrets when this was over.

"I've never been more certain of anything in my entire life."

That was all he needed to hear.

Dante felt remorseful, but he made a choice to live with the guilt and let himself go. He tipped right over the edge of stupidity and allowed it to take him under. Drowning his senses, drowning his fear and his restraint.

Very quickly Dante stopped feeling guilty and forgot how he was supposed to feel and let the sensations come.

But how could he do that when his body burned so badly for her? He stared at her, awed by the sight of her luscious body. She was the most beautiful thing he had ever seen. Her sapphire-blue eyes flared at his frank appraisal. Her look dismantled him, pulling the nails out of the boards of his defenses with those sultry, half-lowered lids.

The pulse of blood in his groin was hot and bounding, and his balls weighed heavy, aching against his thigh.

She reached up to cradle his face in her palms and kissed his lips lightly, sweetly.

He groaned and fisted a hand through her hair.

She nipped at his earlobe, nibbled her way around his chin. He needed a shave, he heard his beard rasp roughly against her skin, but she didn't seem to mind.

"Wait," he said. "We can't do this."

"We've already been over that, Dante. Just be in the moment."

"Can't," he gasped, so aroused he was barely able to speak. "No protection."

"Don't worry." She pulled open the drawer to her bedside table and withdrew a three-pack of condoms. "Got us covered."

"Thank you," he croaked.

"Dante," she breathed huskily, sizing him up with her gaze. "What do you have to brood about, Dante? What dark secret's got you locked up tight?"

She took the index finger of her right hand and pressed it against his sternum. It was as if in that one crystal moment she knew all his secrets and they did not scare her.

The look in her eyes cajoled him. *Come on, you can tell me anything and I promise I won't judge you. Be honest with me.*

But he could not trust that look. Nor his sudden impulse to open his mouth and tell her why he was the way he was. Why he needed control and why sometimes a sharp darkness descended upon him without warning. How a cold hand from the past would unexpectedly clamp down on the nape of his neck and chill him from the inside out. It scared him, the instability of these feelings.

Maybe that was one of the reasons he was so attracted to her. She was so warm, like a cozy fireplace greeting a weary traveler coming in from the cold.

She'd pegged him.

In a rush, it swept through him. His loneliness, his need, his haunting desire for her.

Without preamble, he claimed her mouth with his, surprising them both with the unexpected power.

"Oh," Elle whispered into his mouth and then mumbled, "You taste good."

His rational mind was telling him he shouldn't be doing this, that he was going to regret it as soon as it was over, but his soul was whispering, *Let go, take a chance.*

He closed his eyes. She tasted so sweet and she felt so good in his arms it blanked out all coherent thought. The experience swept over him.

Tongues and mouths and teeth and heat.

He was submerged.

Gone under. Drowning. Happily drowning.

*Fight it.*

He couldn't. He didn't want to fight it. It had been too long and it felt incredible and he was just a man, lonely and looking for a light to lead him in from the blackness.

Abruptly she left the bed.

He opened his eyes, hardly able to focus, his breathing reedy, his mouth tingling.

She stood looking at him, her hair tousled, her chest rising and falling under her fast gasps for breath, her parted lips swollen.

He stood, too, kissed her deep, savoring the heat of her mouth and pulling her up tight to his chest.

Her breasts rubbed against him and he groaned aloud.

Slowly, while trailing both her hands down either side of his body, she sank to her knees.

"Elle," Dante groaned her name when he felt her warm breath against his throbbing skin. "What are you doing?"

"Shh," she said. "Just relax and let me do this."

She was a goddess.

He should tell her to get up, tell her not to do this, tell her that he wanted to be inside her, but he was a man. And when the tip of her tongue flicked out to moisten the head of him, he was a goner one hundred percent.

She splayed her hands across his buttocks. That was a good thing, otherwise he might have toppled over. Her mouth was so sweet. Sweet velvet heat. Her tongue became an instrument of delicious torture.

She'd pushed him to the limits of his endurance. He tried to hold back, tried to resist but he could not. She was too damned wonderful.

Bombs went off in his head.

It felt that powerful. A ball of fire rolled down his body to lodge in the dead center of his aching shaft.

And then he left the earth, shot straight to the stars and it was all her doing.

# 10

HE COLLAPSED BACKWARD onto the bed, pulling her with him. Panting, he closed his eyes, spent, but still wanting more of her. He feared he would never stop wanting her, the hunger was that great. His body stirred, blood pooling between his legs again, making him swell harder than before.

Unbelievable.

Laughing sneakily, Elle curled against his chest.

"Your turn now," he said, once he'd recovered somewhat. "And then we'll see who'll be snickering."

"What?"

He rolled her over onto her back, pinned her to the covers and stared down at her. She was the most incredible sight in the whole wide world, looking up at him with those trusting eyes, nibbling her bottom lip nervously but excited.

Thoroughly, ravenously, he kissed her and she kissed him back with the same starving wildness. Lovemaking had never been like this for him.

Ever.

He wondered if it was special for her, too, or if it was just sex. *Don't think about that. Just be in the moment. Be here with her now.*

He wanted to, but it was so hard letting go.

She pressed her body against his, made a soft moan of desperation low in her throat.

Sensing her need, he began a slow slide from the tender flesh of her breasts to where she most wanted him to go. Trailing kisses down her rib cage to her taut, flat belly, Dante veered to lick the warm, damp path of skin between her legs.

Her thick, womanly scent filled his nostrils as he cradled his head against her thigh. He ran one hand down and then up the opposite leg before tickling higher on the returning stroke.

"Your touch," she whispered. "Incredible."

She shivered as his fingers tiptoed along her skin, tracing his fingernails over the firm curve of her thigh, stopping just short of her sweet inner spot.

His body was on fire for her. Blood pulsed through him, hot and frustrated. He moved his head closer, slightly grazing his lips against her most sensitive skin, and showered her with rich, tender kisses.

His erection was like granite, yearning to plunge deep inside her, but somehow he managed to control himself even though his heart was slamming hard against his chest.

She moaned and arched against his mouth.

His senses swam with each sound she made.

His fingers tangled in her damp curls and he closed his eyes, inhaling her. He kept his eyes shut, knowing her more intimately this way.

He curved his palm over her soft mound and, reaching the spot where her skin began to part, he stroked her gently, allowing his fingers to follow both halves of her. Finally, after she was gasping for air, he slowly sank a finger deep into her feminine folds.

Dante found her moist center engorged with longing.

She moaned earnest and loud, and he almost paused, torturing her sweetly.

"No, no," she said, reading his intentions. "Don't you dare stop."

He thought about it anyway, but he could not be that cruel. Not when she was clinging to his head with both hands and begging, begging for him to take her.

Chuckling, he kissed her, lower and lower. She was a ripe, succulent peach and he was craving her sweet juices.

He put his tongue to her clitoris and it was like switching on a light in a darkened room.

"Yes, yes," she cried. "Exactly. You know exactly where and how to touch me. How do you know that?"

Blind luck was his answer, but he would take whatever gifts he could get. Her responsiveness stoked his ego and tamped down his fear that he might be doing it all wrong. Using two fingers, he moved in slow circles and her hips began to rock gently in response.

He sucked at her every fold, lapping at the ridges, cupping his hands around her buttocks to lift her higher. He made a hungry sound intending for it to hum up through her, vibrate throughout her hooded cleft. It worked. She arched her pelvis upward in reflexive savagery.

"Stunning," she said, letting him know she liked what he was doing to her.

Dante kept it up, giving Elle more of what she needed.

Moaning loudly, she clasped her thighs around him, capturing him against her.

His ears throbbed, obliterating all sounds.

Lightly, he released the suction his hold had on her, but kept his tongue playing across her soft cleft. He toyed with her, wriggling his tongue nimbly around and around until she was breathlessly crying out his name.

Nothing existed for him but Elle's pleasure. He owned every inch of her body. She was his and he was intent on keeping her teetering on the edge.

She made a strangled noise and he knew she was close. So very close. His heart thumped with pride. He was doing this to her and she was loving it.

"I can't stand it any longer," she cried. "I'm going to fly apart."

And then it happened—uncontrollable spasms gripped her body and she shattered against him.

AFTER A THIRTY-MINUTE recovery period, Dante reached for her again with a huge grin on his face.

"Come here."

Elle rolled into his arms, her bare belly pressed against his flat, rippled abdomen. His hard erection pulsed against her outer thigh.

An erotic electricity shot through her entire body when his mouth claimed hers and his hand strayed to explore. His fingers made large circles at the triangle of hair below her navel while his mouth teased hers.

Then his tongue traveled south to the peaks of her jutting breasts. He licked over one nipple, while his thumb rubbed the other straining, aching bud, drawing it into the extraordinary heat of his mouth. His thigh tightened against her leg and his abdominal muscles hardened.

"Dante…" she whispered his name on a sigh. She loved his name. Dante, Dante, Dante. She couldn't say it enough. "Dante, that feels so good."

Her eyes flew open and she lifted her head up off the mattress. She had to see what he was doing. Her gaze latched onto his lips as she watched him drawing her nipple in and out of his mouth.

His tongue laved her sensitive skin as he suckled her deeply. She writhed against him, trying to push her body into his, needing more. Barbed ribbons of fevered sensation unfurled straight to her throbbing sex. Her inner muscles contracted, rollicking with desire for him.

"Dante," she whispered weakly. "Dante."

"Yes, sweetheart. What do you want? Tell me what you need."

"I need you inside me. Now." She looked into his proud face, reached up to trace her finger along his scar and felt something monumental move inside her. It was an emotion unlike anything she'd ever felt before.

She stopped trying to figure out what it was, and just let it sweep her away.

He was kissing her again—her mouth, her nose, her eyelids, her ears. He was over her and around her and then, at last, he was in her.

"Elle," he whispered her name, soft as an ocean breeze, caressing her with sound as he rotated his hips from side to side, maintaining tight, intense contact.

Now, with him deep in her snug wetness, she felt every twitch of his body. He lit her up; a match to gasoline. She had no thoughts beyond wanting him deeper, thrust to the hilt inside of her.

She wrapped her legs around his waist and rocked him into her. Her fingers gripped his buttocks, pushing him further. It was her turn to own him.

Everything was urgent and desperate and frantic. She felt need, such need. To find, to press, to soothe, to fly free.

They came together, and infused, she could not tell where he began and she ended. Their connection was absolute and it filled them in every sense. There was no space for anything else. Their oneness banged through their whole bodies. No moment existed in which they were not part of it, of each other.

She bristled with joy. It felt strong and resilient. It rippled through her body, burning her to a crisp, and she loved it.

When it was over and they were two once more, Elle lay panting in his arms. The total obliteration of what had just happened scared her witless.

The wipeout had been pure. Complete. Unadulterated lust had knocked her into a trance from which she feared there was no awakening.

"YOU KNOW WHAT I JUST realized?" Elle said to Dante a few minutes later. She rolled over onto her side, propped her cheek atop her stacked hands and studied him in the muted evening light seeping through her bedroom window.

"What?" he asked leisurely, lazily shifting his fingers through her hair.

"I barely know anything about you."

His eyes darkened. She could see him mentally pulling away from her as he had that night on the pool table. He was already leaving, packing his bags, trudging his emotional suitcase to the curb.

Suddenly she understood something. Good-looking, successful, accomplished Dr. Dante Nash had never been in love. To test her theory, she asked him the question: "Have you ever been married?"

He didn't answer right away. It looked as if he wasn't going to answer, but then finally, he admitted, "No."

"Ever come close?"

"No."

"Why not? You're rich, handsome, smart."

"I never thought of myself as the marrying kind," he mumbled, bringing her hand to his mouth and gently nibbling her knuckles. It was distracting, the feel of his lips on her skin.

"Why's that?" she asked, determined to find out more about this enigmatic man she'd bedded twice in twenty-four hours.

Dante shrugged. "My work requires all my focus."

"You don't want kids?"

"I want you." He tried to draw her to him again, but she splayed her palm against his chest, keeping him at arm's length.

"Answer the question. Don't you want kids?"

"I suppose I never gave it much thought."

"How can you not have given it much thought?"

"I don't know. I just haven't." He fell back against the pillow, cradled his head in his palms and stared up at the ceiling.

She was losing his attention, but she felt compelled to ask. She was falling for this guy and before she let herself get in too deep, she had to know the answer to the deal-breaking question. If he didn't want children someday, she had to let go of the happily-ever-after fantasy that was starting to curl around her mind.

"How old are you?" she asked.

"Thirty-four."

"And you seriously haven't given kids much thought?"

"No."

"Oh."

"What does that mean."

"Nothing. I just said oh."

"It sounded like you were disappointed."

"Maybe I am."

"And like you were judging me."

"I wasn't."

"But it sounded like it."

"Sounds like you're projecting to me."

He snorted. "We both know too much psychology."

"Hey, you don't know anything about psychology until you've lived with a sociopath psychologist."

"You think Mark is a sociopath?"

"He uses people," she said, "and then he throws them away without the slightest bit of remorse or conscience. I don't want to get mixed up with a guy like that again."

"I'm not like Mark."

"I don't know that. You don't give up much of yourself. How can I know that?" She licked her lips, hating that she sounded halfway desperate.

He studied her and she wished she hadn't gotten on the topic of Mark. "The bastard sure did a number on you. He violated your trust."

Elle lifted her shoulders, tried to look unconcerned. "It's over. I lived to tell the tale. So what about you? Any sordid relationship-gone-wrong stories on your side of the fence?"

"Not really."

"No broken hearts?"

"Sorry, no. Does that disappoint you?"

"It concerns me."

He turned over on his side again and looked surprised. "It does?"

"I'm worried about you. How do you get to the ripe old age of thirty-four without getting your heart broken?"

"Luckily I guess."

*Or unable to love,* she thought sadly.

"I've had my heart broken," she said. "By more than just Mark. In fact, by the time our marriage was over, I realized I had never really loved Mark—I had loved the idea of him. He's got a gift for being what you need him to be. I wanted to warn you, Dante. He's not who you think he is. He's not really your friend. Mark is incapable of caring about anyone but himself."

"Don't worry," he said. "I have no illusions about Mark."

"That's good."

An uncomfortable silence fell between them. Dante shifted and a restless look came into his eyes.

"What do you want, Dante?"

"This." He kissed her, but Elle didn't respond. Already her heart was sinking, certain that he was just the rebound guy. That no matter how much more she might want from him, he wasn't able to give it.

*Let him go,*

The words echoed in her head and she felt sadness to the very center of her bones. Casual sex wasn't all it was cracked up to be. No matter how hard you tried to keep it light, there was always that wistful element. Either guilt or shame or longing for what wasn't ever going to belong to you.

"Elle," he said.

"Yes?" She looked at him, hope—damnable hope—springing into her chest.

"I'm sorry for not being what you want me to be."

Tears burned at the edges of her lids. She bit down on her lip to keep them from flowing over and tracking down her cheeks. "You're exactly what I needed, Dante. I don't want anything else from you than what you've just given me."

That seemed to unsettle him. His jaw tightened. Finally he spoke, "I better head home."

A deep disappointment wound through Elle. He wasn't going to tell her anything important about himself. And because she'd pried, he wasn't even going to stay the night. Part of her wanted to seduce him all over again to get him to stay, but the part of her that had grown stronger after her divorce, the part of her that knew she didn't need a man to be happy, was going to let him get up and walk out the door.

And when he left, when he was gone, the part of her that had secretly hoped for something more, would curl up in bed and let the tears flow.

THIS TIME, DANTE couldn't blame his mistake on Rapture. He had no excuse for his behavior except that Elle had muddled his mind more powerfully than any drug ever invented. He'd never intended on making love to her again, but he had.

Last night had been just about sex, but this afternoon, they had been on the verge of something much more, and frankly, the way she made him feel—strong and secure and loved—had scared the living hell out of him.

Dante couldn't trust these feelings and yet he wanted her more than he wanted to breathe. He wanted to stake his claim, make her his own, but he had no right to do that. Not as long as he was lying to her, investigating her, deceiving her.

He goosed his motorcycle, guiding it down the rain-slicked streets, headed toward the lonely, empty condo he'd rented. Headed away from her warm, loving arms.

*Jackass.*

All she'd wanted from him was a little information, for him to open up and let her in. It wouldn't have taken much. He could have told her about a teenage crush, or shared with her a happy childhood memory, but he had no recollection of those things.

What in the hell was the matter with him? Getting all

soft inside over her, feeling sadness and regret for what could never be.

Technically she was still a suspect.

He was an undercover FBI agent.

They could never mix.

But did he believe it? Not for a minute. And that frightened him more than anything because Dante had never had any problem being suspicious of other people. Yet he wasn't suspicious of Elle. Not anymore. Not after today.

The minute he rolled into the garage, he whipped his cell phone out of his pocket and called Briggins.

"She's not involved," he said the minute his boss answered.

"Excuse me?" Briggins said.

"Elle Kingston. She's not involved in pedaling Rapture."

"I was about to sit down to dinner with my family. This call can't wait until business hours?"

"I don't care if there's a hundred grand of Gambezi's money in her bank account," Dante continued, ignoring what Briggins had said. He was too fired up to apologize for disturbing the man's family dinner. "I'm thinking Mark Lawson planted the money in her account to throw suspicion on Elle. The woman is so trusting I bet she never changed bank accounts after the divorce."

There was silence on the other end of the line.

"Briggins? You still there?"

"Are you, Dante?"

"What's that supposed to mean?"

"You had sex with her."

It wasn't a question. Somehow Briggins knew. Dante pressed a palm to the back of his neck. He wasn't going to acknowledge it. His sex life was none of his boss's business.

"You're letting your feelings for this woman ruin your judgment."

"I'm telling you what I know."

"I've got something to tell you."

"What's that?"

"We had another Rapture death reported. A UT coed on a weekend holiday in Galveston. She downed some Rapture and then took a header off the top floor of the Hotel Galvez. Blood toxicology confirmed it—she had taken Rapture. We've got to stop this scourge. Find me the evidence to connect Gambezi to Mark Lawson and do it fast. Otherwise we'll just have to raid Confidential Rejuvenations and take down Lawson."

"And let Gambezi go free?" The thought appalled him.

"Hey, I've got teenagers. My top priority is getting this drug off the streets," Briggins said.

"You nab that thug Gambezi, then you'll get the drug off the streets."

"My hands are tied on this, Nash. The ball's in your court. Make it happen and make it happen soon, otherwise we're coming in after Lawson."

Briggins was right. It was up to him to connect Gambezi to Mark. "Yes, sir."

"And if your little girlfriend is involved in this, I expect you to arrest her, too."

"She's not involved," he reiterated.

"For your sake," Briggins said, "I hope you're right."

MARK LAWSON WAS GETTING ready for a private party at a well-known Austin actor's house. He studied his reflection in the bathroom mirror. This party wasn't only for pleasure. The actor had promised to hook him up with a Hollywood connection to distribute Rapture. If he could make this work, he could get out from under Gambezi's dirty paws.

And leave Dante and Elle to take the fall while he and Cassandra moved into a Beverly Hills mansion.

He had his ex-wife and his ex-roommate right where he wanted them: tied to the end of the strings he was pulling, and neither one of them had a clue they were being manipulated. He felt like a puppet master, brilliant and powerful.

His cell phone rang, playing his favorite tune, the Rolling Stones' "Sympathy for the Devil." He picked the phone up from the counter, flipped it open and glanced at the caller ID.

Blocked call.

His heart jumped and he knew it was Furio Gambezi.

He let it ring again. No need for the gangster to think that anxiety was pumping blood hard and fast through Mark's veins. Finally, he answered on the fourth ring. "Hello?"

"Lawson." Gambezi's guttural voice sent a chill up his spine.

"Yeah?"

"How's the matter we discussed?"

"Perfect. Great," Mark replied, struggling to keep an optimistic tone in his voice.

"That's not what I've heard."

He was terrified that Gambezi had got word that he was meeting with the Hollywood actor and looking to squeeze out from under the gangster's thumb. "I assure you that the pigeon's been targeted. Give me a couple of days and everything will be good to go."

"You sure?"

"It's covered." In more ways than one.

*By depositing the dirty hundred grand you gave me into my ex-wife's account, killing two birds with one stone.*

"Good, because I've got confirmation."

"Confirmation?"

"The thing I told you? It's true."

Mark frowned. Sometimes he had trouble following Gambezi's cryptic conversations. "Oh, you mean about the fed—"

"Feeding our friends tonight at the steakhouse," Gambezi finished. "I'm ordering filet mignon and you're paying."

For the first time it occurred to Mark that his cell phone might actually be bugged and it wasn't simply a case of Gambezi's paranoia. Was the gangster correct? Were the Feds investigating Confidential Rejuvenations? Had he somehow given himself away?

He thought of the kids who'd overdosed on Rapture, including Pete Russell's son. Was that what had tipped off the Feds? Or could it be Gambezi himself, looking to dispose of Mark so he could get his hands on the formula for Rapture? If he had the formula, Gambezi would no longer need him.

This was why Mark had done what he had done. Taking out extra insurance, turning the tables on Gambezi before the gangster could turn on him. Of course, it meant letting Dante and Elle take the fall, but the way Mark looked at it, better them than him.

"We gotta get this cleaned up," Gambezi instructed. "The sooner the better. I'm gonna send a guy over to your office on Monday with a detailed list of instructions."

"All right," Mark said, thoroughly confused by Gambezi's code. "Instructions about what?"

"Waste disposal."

"Huh?" He'd never get the hang of gangster double-speak.

"Let's just say we're concerned about how the trash has been piling up and you're the new trash collector."

An ominous feeling spread over him and he was suddenly terrified that Gambezi had figured out what he was up to. "Sure, sure, whatever you say."

"And, Lawson?"

"Yeah?"

"You better do as my man suggests or you might find yourself being taken out with the garbage."

# *11*

ON MONDAY MORNING ELLE met Julie and Vanessa for breakfast at the hospital.

"So did everything shake out on Saturday?" Elle asked Vanessa as she settled her tray of fruit, croissant and coffee on the table and took a seat across from her friends.

"You haven't heard?" Vanessa asked.

"What?"

"The cops say it was sabotage," Julie added.

"What was sabotage?" Elle was confused, her mind still on the weekend and her time with Dante.

"Someone not only tampered with the transformer, but with our backup generator, as well." Vanessa leaned back in her chair and took a sip of her coffee with one hand while fidgeting with the red stethoscope around her neck with the other.

"Someone is intentionally trying to harm Confidential Rejuvenations?"

"It sure looks that way. First the media leaks, then the laundry room fire, then the thefts and now this." Vanessa shook her head. "Mark is really concerned. He was here almost all weekend."

That didn't sound like her ex-husband.

"But who would want to do such things?" Julie asked. "And why?"

"Maybe the police will uncover something during their investigation of the generator sabotage." Elle peeled her banana, but suddenly she was no longer in the mood for breakfast.

"Let's forget the doom and gloom," Vanessa said. "How was your weekend, Elle?"

"It was fine." She shrugged, trying to appear nonchalant.

"So how's the mystery lov*er?*" Vanessa teased, putting extra emphasis on the last syllable of the word and dragging it out.

"What mystery lover?" Julie asked.

"The guy from Pete Russell's party. He came by Elle's house on Saturday morning." Vanessa's grin was wicked.

"Did he?" asked Julie, who was always the romantic. Her eyes glowed.

"You made love to him again, didn't you?" Vanessa seemed to be enjoying making her squirm. "I like the way he put a smile on your face. It's been too long since you smiled the way you were on Friday night."

It might not have been a natural smile, Elle thought, becoming more and more convinced that her cosmo had been spiked with some kind of drug. Ultimately, it was the only thing that explained her uncharacteristic behavior at the party.

Feeling her cheeks flush, Elle ducked her head.

"Omigosh," Julie said. "You're falling in love."

Elle winced. She'd lusted after Dante in more ways than one and made some foolish decisions.

"Love?" She tried to laugh off Julie's comment. "What makes you think I'm falling in love?"

Julie's bright eyes twinkled. "It's all over you."

Elle took a big gulp of her latte to keep from answering. Julie was always on the lookout for romance, both for herself and for her friends.

But love?

Come on. Elle didn't love Dante any more than he loved her. They shared chemistry, yes. They were attracted to each other, and he challenged her in ways no man had ever challenged her before.

But *love?*

Dante had given her delicious orgasms, but when it was over, he'd walked away without a whisper of anything more between them.

At the same time, she was the one who'd told him that he was nothing more than a fling. How else could she have expected him to react?

Elle stared at her coffee cup, recalling the way her arms had felt wrapped tight around his waist as they'd traveled down the rain-slick road on his motorcycle.

"So tell me, Jules, just what does love look like?" she asked, trying not to sound sarcastic, but she was afraid she'd been unsuccessful.

"It makes your cheeks turn red and it makes you nibble your lip like you're in trouble and it brings a secret smile to your face when you think no one is looking."

"Is it possible," Elle whispered, "to be in love and not know it?"

Julie gave her an enigmatic look. "You'll know the truth deep inside if you just get quiet and listen to your heart."

Vanessa snorted.

"You have no faith." Julie shook her head sadly.

Unable to bear the conversation one minute longer, Elle finished her breakfast quickly and made her excuses to her girlfriends. She had a lot of things to do that day—staff scheduling, chart reviews and E.D. supply inventory.

And to totally forget that she could very well be falling in love with Dante Nash.

ON HER WAY TO HER OFFICE, Elle took a detour through the E.D. to check up on things. Then she spied Dante standing in the work lane looking regal as ever in his suit and tie. Her heart did a back flip. She hadn't seen him since he'd left her place on Saturday night.

Their eyes met.

How could she stop thinking about him when she'd be seeing him every single day? Seeing him and wanting him. Remembering how his body felt inside of hers.

She stared at his lips. How she would love to have his mouth on hers again, his hands in her hair, his big body pressed into her. But he was the one who'd walked away. He was the one who'd left in the middle of the night.

"Elle," he murmured, his eyes never leaving her face.

She didn't know how to respond. Part of her wanted to fling herself in his arms and not care if anyone saw her. Another part of her, however, was loath to let him see how much he'd gotten to her, how much she cared, how scared she was to love again.

Briskly she nodded. "Dr. Nash."

He blinked, pressed his lips into a straight line. "So it's Dr. Nash now?"

"Under the circumstances I think it's best if we keep things totally professional," she said, stiffening her shoulders, fighting the scary feelings battering her heart.

"I don't agree."

Her restless pulse stilled. "No?"

"No."

She arched an eyebrow, clinging to her guard even as

she was longing to let it down again. Oh, she was weak and foolish.

He cleared his throat, loosened his tie. "I know there are things I need to say. Things you need to hear."

"I have no expectations of you." She kept her expression neutral, but her insides were in turmoil.

"Maybe not, but I have expectations of myself. This is difficult for me. I'm not good at expressing my emotions but I'm working on it. Can you give me some time? There's something I need to settle before I can tell you what I need to tell you most."

She nodded, unable to speak because her throat was so clotted with emotion.

They stood there staring at each other, neither moving.

"Well," she said, feeling as if she was hanging over a cliff, waiting to free fall to the bottom. "I have work to attend to."

"I do, as well."

They both started to move at once and ended up blocking each other in the doorway. She moved left at the exact moment Dante shifted in the same direction. She went right and so did he.

She felt a flustered heat rise up her throat.

He reached out and touched her shoulder. "You stay put, I'll go."

He did just that, and as Elle watched him leave, she felt all the energy drain from her body. It took so much darn effort to control herself when she was near him. Quickly, she glanced over her shoulder to see if anyone had noticed her odd encounter with Dante, but thankfully, there was no one else around.

When she saw she wasn't being observed, she darted her gaze back in Dante's direction and watched him walk away with a sigh, a mixture of yearning and sadness mucking around inside her.

He did have a mighty fine butt.

Resolutely she shook off the thought and headed into her office, trying to figure out if this hold the man had on her was just lust or something else entirely.

AFTER HIS ENCOUNTER with Elle in the E.D. Dante headed out the back exit of the hospital and followed the stone walkway over to the doctors' building. The morning sun was warm on his face, but his heart was anything but light.

He had thought that seeing Elle would make him feel better about the way they'd left things between them.

It had not.

He'd taken her to bed knowing he was going to end up hurting her. What he hadn't counted on was how miserable he felt about it. Elle was a good woman. She deserved so much better than what he could give.

"Morning Dr. D.," Hailey greeted him as he walked through the door. "Wasn't Pete Russell's party awesome?"

Before he could answer her, the hospital intercom went off.

"Code Silver, E.D. Code Silver, E.D. Code Silver, E.D."

Code Silver?

Code Silver meant there was a hostage situation in the emergency department.

Elle!

Pivoting on his heel, he turned and rushed back the way he'd come, his temples pounding, pulse racing. Seconds later, he rounded the hospital corridor leading to the E.D.

The hallway was completely empty, no one in sight.

Everyone had taken cover or got their patients outside to safety as part of the Code Silver protocol.

In the distance, he heard the wail of sirens. The cops were on the way.

The scene was eerily reminiscent of his first day on the job, but that situation had been a disaster drill. This was real.

Without a thought for his own safety, Dante strode through the double doors and into the work lane. Papers were strewn across the room, equipment knocked over, glass lay shattered on the floor.

Several of the E.D. nurses and Maxine Woodbury stood huddled in the corner by the front desk. A cold splash of reality followed by the bracing slap of adrenaline, doused him like ice water in the face. The air in his lungs turned turgid and his blood drummed heavily though his ears.

There was Elle, her neck caught in the crook of a young man's elbow. His eyes were wild, pupils dilated; his mused hair stood straight up on his head. In his other hand, he held a gleaming scalpel against Elle's carotid artery.

True terror seized Dante. Even without meaning to, the drug-crazed kid could kill her. One slip of the knife and she was dead.

Dante thought about the gun hidden in the ankle holster beneath his silk suit, but he knew he wouldn't have a chance to go for it.

"Stay away," the young man threatened, his gaze flashing from the huddled nurses to Dante. "Or I'll slice her throat wide open."

Anger gripped Dante, replacing his terror. Rage furrowed his brow, tightening the corners of his mouth and narrowing his eyes. He was ensnared in the grip of his old but dangerous friend once more. Fury, pure and clean and trustworthy.

He fisted his hands, cocked his knees, ready to spring. And then his eyes met Elle's.

*No,* she mouthed silently and her serene energy seemed to snap through the work lane and enter his body.

Holding her steady gaze, a strange sense of calm pushed aside his anger. Dante remembered what she'd told him the very day they'd met, right here, in this very spot, during her mock disaster drill.

He knew what he had to do.

"What's your name?" Dante asked.

"None of your damn business," the young man replied.

"It's Greg," whispered nurse Jenny Lucas. "Greg Browning."

"It's okay, Greg." He raised both hands, and swung his attention from Elle to the crazed young man. Everything in Dante wanted just to spring at the kid and disarm him the way he'd disarmed the orderly Ricky on his first day, but he could not risk it. Not with Elle's life at stake. He had to control his anger and put himself in Greg Browning's shoes and show the kid a little empathy.

"No one's going to hurt you," Dante said in the most soothing voice he could muster.

"She was." The kid tightened his grip on Elle's neck. "She was gonna take away my high."

"Desocan," said one of the nurses huddled in the corner between Dante and the disturbed patient. "She was trying to give him Desocan."

"I just wanna make love," the kid said, lightly stroking Elle's throat with the tip of the scalpel. "And she wanted to stop me."

"No one's going to give you anything you don't want."

Dante said. "Please, put the knife down. You don't want to hurt anyone. I can tell you're a good person."

Outside the hospital, the sirens screeched to a halt.

"The cops!" The kid's glassy-eyed stare shot wildly toward the door. "They're going to take me to jail."

"Not if you put down the knife," Dante said evenly. "We'll tell them it was all a misunderstanding. That we were having a disaster drill and role-playing a hostage situation and someone misunderstood."

"You'd do that?" The kid looked as though he desperately wanted to trust someone.

Dante dared to inch a step closer and the kid tolerated it. He had to defuse the situation before the cops came through that door, or the kid could very easily slit Elle's throat out of panic and fear. Dante didn't have much time.

"Listen to me, Greg. We know that you got hold of some bad designer drug—it's happening to a lot of people. We know you didn't mean to cause any trouble. Please don't do anything to make things worse for yourself."

Dante took another step forward.

Greg darted his gaze back and forth from Dante to the door, desperate for a way out.

"Let her go," Dante prompted softly.

"I…I…"

"Your thinking is a little cloudy. Everything feels distorted. You're floating. Not sure if what you're feeling is real or not."

The kid nodded.

"I understand." Another step, and then another. Dante was almost there, but he couldn't rush it and yet he couldn't wait too long.

"I was where you were once—young, confused, mixed up with the wrong crowd—but look at me. I turned away from that path and now I'm a doctor. This can all go away. You can have a fresh start. Please, just put down the knife."

The kid's hand trembled and he relaxed his grip on Elle's throat.

That was all Dante needed.

One long-legged stride and he was at the young man's side, wrapping the fingers of his left hand around the hostage taker's wrist in a viselike grip. "Drop the scalpel," he murmured, just as the SWAT team burst through the door into the E.D.

Startled, the kid jumped back and ended up slicing the scalpel across the middle of Dante's right palm.

Blood bloomed across Dante's white lab coat but he didn't even see it—his eyes were focused on Elle.

"Run," he yelled as Browning spun after her.

The SWAT team tackled the kid.

Dante's knees swayed.

The next thing he knew he was lying on the floor looking up into the dearest face he had ever seen.

Elle.

She hadn't run away.

"YOU WERE EXTREMELY BRAVE," Elle said. She was perched on a rolling stool beside the gurney in exam room one, where Dante sat having his palm stitched up by Dr. Butler. He refused to lie back against the pillow; he felt stupid enough getting shocked from having his hand sliced opened. "You saved my life."

She looked proud and worried and so beautiful that his belly burned from wanting her.

"You should have run when I told you to," he said.

"You're not the boss of me, Dante Nash." She squeezed his left hand and her touch felt so damned good he had to clench his jaw to keep from thinking ridiculous thoughts. Like how nice it would be to always have her hand to hold on to.

"Why did you stay?"

"You needed me."

"What I needed was for you to get away."

"The kid didn't mean me any real harm and I knew it. He was just scared. If SWAT hadn't interrupted when they did, you would have talked him into surrendering his knife."

"They had no way of knowing what the situation was." Dante felt compelled to take up for the SWAT team.

"They were too gung-ho." Elle frowned.

"All's well that ends well," Butler said. "The young man has been admitted into the rehab center and he's getting the help he needs. No one lost their life. That's the important thing."

"Dante got sliced up," Elle said.

"The wound's deep," Butler agreed, "but it didn't nick any tendons. You might have trouble zipping up your pants for several weeks and you won't be doing surgery anytime soon, but you'll make a full recovery."

Butler tied off the last stitch and snipped the thread. "I'll write you a prescription for pain pills and have the pharmacy fill it." Butler stood and headed for the door. He stopped in the entryway, turned back and said, "I want you to go home."

Dante had no intention of going home. He had only one thing on his mind—getting that damned Rapture off the streets and putting Mark and Gambezi behind bars. They were the two who were really responsible for what had happened to Greg Browning.

Dante had his game plan mapped out. He'd outfitted

himself with a wire, and he'd been in the process of hunting down Mark when the Code Silver had interrupted. He'd been planning to saunter into Mark's office, tell him how much he liked Rapture and that he wanted in on the action. The wire was still taped to his chest. All he'd have to do was flick the button to the recording device in his pants to record when he was ready. It was past time to make a move.

Once Butler had left the room, Elle smiled at him and touched his forearm. "I'm so proud of you."

*It was all because of you,* he thought, but didn't say it.

"When I saw he had you by the neck…" Dante let his words trail off, unable to voice his fears.

"I'll get someone to cover for me here," Elle said, "and I'll drive you home."

"No," he said sharply.

She looked crestfallen and he realized he'd hurt her feelings. "Okay. I'll find someone else to drive you home."

"I'm not going home."

"You can't work with that injury." She indicated his hand. It bore a deep cut from the outer edge of his index finger through the fatty part of his palm to his wrist. It throbbed like three shades of hell, but Dante didn't care. He would suck up the pain and do his job.

"I can do dictation," he said for her benefit. "Make rounds."

"All right," she said. "Do what you have to do."

Dante left the E.D. and went back across the courtyard. Mark was pulling into his parking space just as Dante reached the office. He stuck his hand in his pocket to switch on the tiny recorder connected to the hidden microphone.

"Dante," Mark called out, stopping him before he went into the building.

"Mark."

Lawson dropped his gaze to Dante's bandaged hand. "What happened, man?"

He told him what had transpired in the E.D.

"No kidding?"

"They admitted Browning to drug rehab."

"Heavy duty."

"Yeah, heavy duty," Dante echoed.

Mark shifted his weight, linked his arms over his chest. Dante watched him closely, but tried to keep his face neutral. "So how was Friday night?" Mark asked.

"It was," Dante said cautiously, "an education."

A sly smile crossed Mark's face. "Anything interesting pop up?"

"As a matter of fact, I wanted to discuss that very thing with you. The evening turned quite interesting indeed."

Mark glanced over his shoulder, scanned the parking lot. "Why don't we go someplace a little more private?"

Dante's heart rate kicked up, sending a fresh rush of blood to his aching palm, but he ignored the pain. "Inside?"

"I was thinking you might like to see my lab."

"Where you compound the Rapture?"

"That's right."

"It's here? At Confidential Rejuvenations?"

Mark nodded. "Come with me."

He started out across the path that led into the woods where Dante had followed Elle on his first day at the hospital.

"It's out here?"

"The old sanctuary," Mark said.

An ominous feeling spread over Dante as his ex-roommate motioned for Dante to go ahead of him. "Straight down that path to where it diverges."

His gut was telling him to get the hell out of there. Why

was Mark behind him? Did he suspect something? The thought racked his nerves.

"So how was your Rapture ride?" Mark asked.

"Impressive." Every muscle in Dante's body was coiled tightly.

They arrived at the fork in the path. Dante stopped, looked over his shoulder at Mark, whose face was cloaked in shadows. He couldn't shake the ominous feeling that things were about to go very bad.

"Take a left." Mark indicated the path that sank deeper into the forest with a nod.

Dante went left. The trees were thicker here, entirely blotting out the sun. The air was cooler, as well, the drop in temperature menacing.

"Did you hook up with anyone special?" Mark asked, sounding strangely gleeful.

Dante made an appreciative noise for Mark's benefit. "Oh, yeah."

"Who was it?"

Dante ducked beneath a low-hanging oak tree branch and slanted another look back. Mark had his right hand jammed in his pocket and it looked as if he was clutching something in his fist.

The lump in Dante's throat tightened. Was it a gun?

A gun seemed like a bold, unnecessary move on Mark's part. Unless he was feeling threatened. Unless he'd guessed the truth and he was prepared to kill to protect his stash of Rapture.

"A gentleman doesn't kiss and tell," Dante said lightly, walking deeper into the forest. Up ahead, he spied a round, domed building with darkly tinted windows. There was the acrid smell of chemicals in the air. Dante's nose twitched.

"Was it Elle?"

Mark's words turned his blood icy and his injured palm, which seconds before had been throbbing with pain, went suddenly numb. "Elle?"

"I know you're attracted to her. Don't think I haven't noticed the way you look at her."

"Why would you think it was Elle?" Dante asked. "Surely you know she's not the kind of woman who would act so rashly."

A smirk crossed Mark's face. "Because I put a tab of Rapture in Elle's drink the night of the party. She was feeling just as horny as you were. So what did you think?"

Anger drained the color from his face and formed a hard knot in the pit of his stomach. Instinct had him clenching his fist, but the tight stitches in his palm stopped the motion. At that moment, more than anything else, he wanted to knock Mark in the dirt.

But he couldn't do that. He had to act as if he approved. He was within inches of being shown the laboratory where Mark concocted his dangerous drug. Soon now, very soon, he'd have his revenge against Gambezi, as long as he didn't jump the gun and arrest Mark prematurely. The Feds needed hard evidence to make the case against Gambezi stick. If Dante arrested Mark now, even if Mark gave up Gambezi, it would just be Mark's word against the gangster's. What Dante needed was clear physical evidence that Gambezi was in on it with Mark.

This was the end of the line. He was going to have to lie and he was going to have to make it sound convincing. The taste of it was bitter on his tongue, but he had no choice. It had to be done.

"She was one fine horny piece of ass," Dante forced the crude, ugly words from his mouth even though it twisted him up inside to have to say them about her. "How come you gave up tapping that?"

Mark slapped him on the shoulder and chortled. "Apparently she's much better under the influence of Rapture. I didn't have the pleasure of using it on her when we were married. I just got the formula down pat over the past six months. Come on, let me show it to you."

# *12*

IN THE AFTERMATH of the hostage-taking situation, Elle couldn't concentrate. She stood at her office window, looking out at the rolling grounds and trying to sort out her feelings for Dante, when she spied him and Mark walking into the forest together.

What were they up to?

Curiosity and a heavy trepidation she couldn't identify had her telling Maxine she was taking a break. She slipped outside, heading in the direction Mark and Dante had gone.

She walked carefully, making sure not to break any twigs on the stone path and give away her presence. Her pulse was pounding so loudly it seemed to fill up her ears. She took a deep breath of the spring air heavy with pollen and the scent of honeysuckle.

When she came to the fork in the path, she could hear muffled voices to the left, although she could not make out what they were saying. It appeared as if Dante and Mark were headed toward the old sanctuary.

What was this all about?

She went after them, moving as quietly as she could, guiltily admitting to herself that she was hoping to overhear their conversation without them discovering that she was sneaking up behind them.

With the thick undergrowth springing out across the neglected path, it was easy to stay hidden. She eased behind oak trees, cloaked herself in the long, slender branches of weeping willows.

The men were almost to the sanctuary when the wind changed and she could finally hear their conversations. Elle cocked her head, straining to listen. What came out of her ex-husband's mouth chilled her through to the core of her soul.

"Because I put a tab of Rapture in Elle's drink the night of the party. She was feeling just as horny as you were. So what did you think?"

It all made sense now. The bitter-tasting cosmopolitan, the way she had felt all sensuous and uncontrollably aroused, how she'd lost her head and succumbed to sex with Dante on the pool table. Her stomach roiled and she placed a hand to her mouth, fought back nausea.

And then Dante said something that hurt a thousand times more than anything Mark said.

"She was one fine horny piece of ass."

Lies. It had all been lies. Her marriage to Mark. Her feelings for Dante. She felt as if she'd been drugged her entire life and was just now having her eyes open to the cruel ways of the world.

Everything inside Elle fractured. Utterly broken, she sucked in her breath and clutched a hand to her belly.

She heard the creak of a hinge as the outer door to the sanctuary opened then swung closed again as Mark and Dante stepped inside.

Hurt and confusion settled over her, dark as a tornado cloud. The blood rushed to her head and her eyesight dimmed. Compelled by a madness she could not explain, she forced herself forward, desperate to hear more of their horrible conversation.

She'd done it again, Elle realized. Trusted too much, loved too quickly, fallen for the wrong man. She'd made love with Dante and the hot chemistry between them had been nothing more than the effects of a sex drug her ex-husband had engineered. None of what she'd felt for Dante was real. It was all an illusion.

*What about after the softball game? You weren't under influence of a drug then. And honestly, hadn't the sex on Saturday night been better than the drug-induced sex?*

It had, but that was beside the point. It was still just sex. Nothing meaningful. No real intimacy. She was a "piece of ass," as Dante so eloquently put it. The point was she'd been drugged and Dante thought of her as nothing more than an easy conquest.

Her body trembled and the sour taste of bile rose into her mouth. It was all she could do to keep from throwing up. She should have known better. She *had* known, and yet she'd foolishly allowed herself to fall for him anyway.

She felt like such a fool.

*Don't jump to conclusions. It could just be guy talk.*

She wanted so much to believe that he was only boasting for Mark's sake, but she'd been burned before.

In her mind's eye she saw Dante as he'd looked that morning, standing in the E.D. work lane, telling her with his eyes what he could not say with his words. That he wanted her, he cared for her, but he didn't know how to tell her. He'd appeared so earnest then, so vulnerable.

*Give him the benefit of the doubt.*

What? And hand him the opportunity to hurt her all over again? No thank you. She'd turn around, go back to the hospital and forget all about Dante Nash.

But she could not.

Compelled by a force that she could neither explain nor control, she crept up to the sanctuary.

*Go back, get out of here. Leave Dante and Mark to their dark business.*

But she did not heed her own advice. Closer and closer she crept until she was standing under one of the boarded-up windows in the front. Standing up on her tiptoes, she tried to peer through a small slit between the boards.

Nose smashed against the plywood, one eye closed as she squinted, Elle's mind was so absorbed in trying to see what was beyond that tinted glass, she did not hear the footsteps sneaking up behind her until it was too late to run.

THEY WALKED INTO the dark, windowless basement of the sanctuary. Mark flicked on the overhead fluorescent lights as they went. Dante tensed when he saw it—the vented hoods where the drugs were mixed and com-pounded, the room where they were pressed and molded into oblong tablets. The chemical smell was stronger in here. Seeing the staggering amount of packaged yellow pills laid out in bins ready for distribution sent a chill straight through Dante.

"This is where the magic happens," Mark said. "Where we take chemicals and turn them into pure sensual pleasure just waiting to be swallowed."

*Stay cool, stay calm, ask him about his distribution channels. Get him to tell you about Gambezi.*

"We? You're not doing this on your own?"

"I have a backer."

"Will I meet this backer?"

"There's no need for that."

"How do you get—" Dante began but got no further.

A clattering outside drew their attention toward the door.

Hearing a shuffling noise and then a thud, Dante spun on his heels in time to see Gambezi, that disgusting rodent of a man, dragging a body with him into the underground room.

His heart stopped when he saw the cascade of auburn curls falling over Gambezi's arm.

Elle.

His horrified gaze fixed on her lifeless body. Was she dead?

Abject panic, raging fury and raw grief assailed him all at once. The last time he'd felt like this was the day he'd learned Leeza had been found murdered.

He didn't think. He couldn't think. All the anger and revenge he'd been holding inside for the past three years came spewing out of him like hot molten venom from the very depths of hell.

"You bastard," he yelled and launched himself at Gambezi. "What have you done to her?"

Before he could reach Gambezi, the man stuck a snub-nose thirty-eight in his face. "Back off, tough guy. You can't save her with a bullet in your brain."

"She's alive?" Dante dropped to his knees where Elle lay unconscious on the floor. His eyes were on her face, assessing her. Her breathing was shallow, her skin cool to the touch, her lips ashen. He saw a wicked-looking knot rising on her temple and from the impact marks, knew Gambezi must have hit her with the thirty-eight.

*Don't let your anger cause you to do something stupid. Elle's life is at stake. She's counting on you. Stay in control and think. Think.*

"For now," Gambezi said. "As long as you mind your manners."

"What's going on?" Mark asked with a bewildered tone in his voice. "What's this about? Dante's the partner I was telling you about. He's throwing in with us."

"I'll tell you what's going on, genius," Gambezi said with disgust. "The patsy you picked to frame is an undercover FBI agent."

"What?" Mark's eyes widened and his Adam's apple bobbed.

"That's right. Go ahead and ask him."

Mark swung his gaze to Dante. Sweat was popping out all over the man's brow. "Is that true?"

Dante raised his head, clenched his jaw and stared Mark down. "It's true."

Mark's color turned white as cotton.

"He's a government man," Gambezi said. "Now you're going to straighten this mess out."

"Me?"

"You caused it. He's your buddy. You'll have to get your hands dirty, doctor boy." Gambezi pulled thick zip ties from his back pocket and tossed them at Mark. "Tie them up."

Dante's mind whirled as he estimated the distance between himself and Gambezi. He thought of his gun nestled in his ankle holster, but he wouldn't be able to reach for it before Gambezi squeezed off a shot. And he had no doubt the gangster was very good with a gun. Not that Dante was afraid to die—he'd gladly take a bullet if he could kill the bastard in the process. What he couldn't do was die and leave Elle to fend for herself.

Mark came toward him with the zip ties.

"Don't do this, Mark. Gambezi is the one we really want. Turn against him. The D.A.'s office will offer you a sweet plea bargain to nail him."

Mark didn't hesitate. "Put your hands behind your back."

Reluctantly Dante did so.

Mark bent behind him and secured the zip ties tight around his wrists. "I can't," he whispered in Dante's ear. "Gambezi is a psycho. He'll kill me as quick as he'll kill you."

"Right you are, Mark, so stop whispering and get busy. Now the girl."

"She's out cold."

"Do it anyway," Gambezi said, twirling the thirty-eight like some gunslinger from a spaghetti western.

Mark pulled Elle's arms around, rested them on her stomach and zip tied them together. When he was finished, he stood up.

Abruptly Gambezi stopped twirling, palmed the gun and shot Mark in the dead center of his chest.

He fell back, staggering with a desperate, gasping, bone-chilling moan. Dante's gut clenched as he heard the hard, heavy thud of Mark's body hitting the ground.

But his eyes were fixed on Gambezi like a mongoose's on a cobra.

"That takes care of the plea bargain," Gambezi said. "Now, you, get over there in the corner." He waved the gun at Dante.

Dante got to his feet, bracing himself for the bullet he knew was coming. But once he was in the corner, Gambezi walked away from him, stepped over Elle and avoided the spreading pool of Mark's blood. He closed and locked the door behind him.

Dante's head spun dizzily, and it was only then he realized he'd been holding his breath. Why hadn't Gambezi killed them?

He heard a soft moan, saw Elle move.

Her eyelids fluttered open. "Dante?"

"Elle?" He could hear the joy crack his voice. He went to her immediately. "Are you all right?"

Wincing, she struggled to sit up. "What's happening?"

"Furio Gambezi knocked you out and dragged you in here."

"Who's Furio Gambezi?"

"He's been distributing the designer street drugs that were responsible for what happened to Travis Russell and Greg Browning and many more. Your ex-husband's been using this place to manufacture the drug they call Rapture."

"And you?" she whispered. "Are you his business partner?"

"Elle," he said. "I'm with the FBI."

"Really?" Her eyes softened and she sounded relieved. "I overheard you talking, and I thought the most horrible things about you."

"I know what you thought, but I'm not helping Mark make Rapture. I'm investigating him and Furio Gambezi."

Her laugh was shaky.

He glanced around the room, looking for some kind of tool he could use to cut through the zip ties and get them out of this.

"Dante," she said again.

"Uh-huh."

"Can you hear that?"

"Hear what?" He spied a pill cutter on the counter and headed for it.

"That ticking noise."

"What ticking noise?" He cocked his head and strained to hear what she was hearing.

"I dunno," she said, "but it sounds sort of like a bomb to me."

ELLE'S TEMPLE WAS throbbing and she couldn't seem to wrap her brain around what was happening. She didn't remember anything from the time she'd been whacked on the temple to the moment she'd regained consciousness in the sanctuary.

Now she was trying to digest the fact that she and Dante had been locked in this basement where Mark concocted a designer drug for some criminal. Who apparently had also set off a bomb to blow them to smithereens.

But in spite of everything, deep down inside she was feeling ridiculously, inexplicably giddy. Dante wasn't a drug dealer. He was undercover with the FBI.

"So that's why he didn't shoot us," Dante said. "He intended on destroying the lab and us along with it."

"There's blood," Elle gasped, seeing it for the first time on the floor beside her. "Dante, are you hurt?"

"It's not my blood," he said at the exact second she noticed the body.

Her eyes met his. "Who?"

"I'm afraid it's Mark."

"Is he…?"

"Gambezi shot him in the chest."

She gasped as the thought registered completely, but the clock was ticking down to their doom. They had to find a way out of there, and fast.

"Here," Dante said, crossing the room toward her, hands tied behind his back. "I've got a pill cutter. See if you can get these zip ties off me."

He turned his back to her, sank down on his knees in front of her. It wasn't easy for her to free him with the zip ties binding her own wrists. Repeatedly she bumped into his bandaged hand, still raw with fresh stitches. He bit back groans of pain. After several clumsy attempts she was finally able to saw through the thick plastic zip ties with the sharp edge of the pill cutter.

Once Dante was free, he cut Elle loose. She wrung her hands, gone aching and white from lack of circulation, to get the blood flowing again. Gently he helped her to her feet.

"Don't worry about me, get to the bomb," she said.

Simultaneously they bolted for the closet door from where the ticking sound came. Their hands reached for the knob at the same time, but Dante got there first.

Elle's hand clamped down over his. "We're in this together."

He looked at her. Nodded. They turned the knob at the same time.

It did not budge.

Locked.

Dante cursed. He had no doubt that either Mark or Gambezi had hidden the bomb for such an eventuality as this and that Gambezi had activated it remotely. Surely only a very few minutes would have been programmed on the timer. Just long enough for Gambezi to get clear of Confidential Rejuvenations and provide himself with an alibi before the bomb detonated. Dante figured they had thirty minutes tops.

Desperately he searched for something to use as a battering ram. But there was nothing, and besides, he didn't know how unstable the detonation device was. Okay, brute force was out, so how about something to pick the lock with?

"Wait," Elle said. "I've got an idea."

Her calmness surprised him, but it shouldn't have. She'd always shown grace under pressure and he admired her for it more than he could ever say.

"What is it?"

"Try the top of the door frame. That's where Mark used to hide the key at our house."

"Ditto in our college dorm room."

"Not very original," Elle said as Dante reached up to run his fingers over the top of the door frame.

"Pay dirt." He held up the key for her to see. "Thank God for his lack of imagination."

Dante tried to stick the key into the lock, but his right hand was hurting so badly, he fumbled the key and dropped it.

"Here," Elle said, picking it up. "Let me." She inserted the key into the lock and turned it.

Dante pulled the door open.

They saw the bomb sitting on the middle shelf, attached to a timer, counting down with a resounding click.

When Dante saw the red neon numbers, his breath left his body. They had exactly five minutes and twenty-two seconds to defuse the bomb.

"WE'RE GOING TO DIE," Elle said quietly, simply, as if she'd already made peace with their fate.

"No. No we're not."

"I appreciate your optimism, Dante, but there's no way we can get out of here in five minutes."

"I'm going to defuse the bomb." He pulled his cell phone from his pocket with his left hand and called Briggins to tell him what had happened.

"I'll get a team together immediately," Briggins said. "We'll get over there right away. You hang on while I patch you through to the bomb squad."

"Hurry," Dante shouted. "We've only got four minutes left."

It took thirty seconds to get the bomb squad on the phone to talk him through defusing the bomb.

"What kind of equipment do you have? Wire snips? A knife?" asked the bomb squad guy who said his name was Fred.

"A pill cutter."

"That's it?"

"Yeah."

"If that's all you've got, then that's all you've got."

"Wait, I have bandage scissors from when I was trimming your dressing," Elle said and pulled the scissors from her pocket.

Dante relayed this new info to the bomb squad guy.

"Okay, great, let's go," said Fred.

Dante took the bandage scissors from Elle and promptly dropped them.

Elle picked them up. She stood to face him. "I'm going to have to do this. You're in no shape for this with your hand."

"No," he said adamantly.

"You can't protect me. You might as well let me try. I have a better chance of pulling this off than you do. Let Fred talk you through it and then you can relay the info to me. But we better do something fast because we only have two minutes left!"

She was right. He couldn't hold the damn scissors in his right hand and his left hand wasn't adept enough to perform the delicate maneuvers.

"I know you're used to being in control, Dante, but you're just going to have to trust me on this."

Trust.

Something he'd never been able to do.

"Describe the bomb to me," Fred was saying in his ear.

Dante swallowed and described the bomb.

"It's simple. Easy to defuse," Fred blurted, "but it's volatile. The slightest jostle could detonate it."

Dante blew out his breath.

"What he'd say?" Elle asked, bandage scissors posed over the wires.

Her bravery touched something deep inside of him. He wished he could spare her this. Wished he could take the brunt of her burden.

"Elle," he said.

"Yes?"

Their eyes met, held.

"I trust you."

Her grin widened. She looked as if he'd just told her she was the most beautiful woman on the face of the earth. "Thank you for that," she said.

"Tell her to snip the green wire," Fred said.

"Green wire," Dante relayed to Elle.

Every muscle in his body turned to stone. He felt useless, standing here with the phone pressed to his ear while Elle carefully leaned in over the bomb. The clock ticked louder and louder until it sounded like a jet engine roaring through his ears.

Sixty seconds left.

"He's sure it's the green wire?" Elle breathed as she slipped the jaws of the cuticle scissors around the green wire.

"You sure it's the green wire?" Dante asked Fred.

"Tell me about the configuration again."

Dante did.

"It's the green wire."

"He says it's the green wire."

Forty seconds left.

She looked over at Dante. "Here goes," she said. "If we

don't make it out of here alive, just know this. I love you, Dante Nash."

And with that, Elle brought the scissors down on the green wire.

THE WIRE DIDN'T break.

Panic seized her. Sweat beaded her brow and her upper lip. Elle pressed down as hard as she could on the bandage scissors.

The wire was too thick!

Twenty seconds left.

Panic took hold of her then. Wildly, she stared at the neon-red glow of the clock timer.

Nineteen seconds.

"Try again," Dante said calmly. "You can do this."

Eighteen seconds.

The room seemed to spin. Her temple throbbed with each push of blood through her veins. Regret filled her heart. She couldn't breathe. They were going to die before they ever really got to know each other.

"Pay no attention to the clock," Dante instructed. "It's just you and me here, babe, and I trust you with my life."

His words bolstered her courage. She opened the scissors. They'd made a groove in the copper wiring. Gently she slid the scissors farther up on the wire, getting it to the very back of the scissors for a stronger bite. If this didn't work…

No, she couldn't afford to think like that. It had to work.

Ten seconds.

"Here goes." She grit her teeth and gripped down on the scissors as hard as she could.

The wire snapped.

The timer stopped counting down.

Total silence.

Then Dante let out of whoop of triumph. "She did it, Fred, she did it."

Elle joyously flung herself into Dante's waiting arms. He spun her around in circles.

It had never felt so great to be alive.

# 13

SEVERAL MINUTES LATER, Briggins and his team busted through the locked laboratory door to find Dante sitting on the floor, Elle in his lap, her arms wrapped around his neck while he stroked her hair. He held her to him, her sweet scent filling his nostrils. Nothing had ever smelled so wonderful.

Briggins hesitated at the door. "You okay?" he asked, scanning the room with his gun drawn.

Dante nodded. "We're fine."

Briggins holstered his gun and the rest of the team stepped across the threshold with him. Another agent went directly to the lifeless body on the floor.

"Lawson?" Dante mouthed silently to Briggins.

His boss shook his head.

Dante saw the somber expression on his boss's face. "Gambezi?"

"He disappeared from his penthouse—place is empty. But we've got enough to nail him when he resurfaces. The important thing is, you shut down the Rapture factory." Briggins swept a hand at the room.

As they were talking, the agents scurried around, bagging and tagging the pills and equipment as evidence.

Dante expected to feel angry that Gambezi had gotten away, but he couldn't rouse any rage. He was just happy to be alive and with Elle.

Briggins was right. The important thing was they were taking the drug off the black market. Sooner or later, they'd get Gambezi. Dante no longer felt that nabbing the gangster was his own personal vendetta. He realized now he couldn't control everything, that he wasn't in charge of all the justice in the world. It was a humbling, and freeing, realization.

Something had changed in him, and he wasn't sure what—or why—but he felt good. Better than he should. And a whole lot of it had to do with the woman clutched tightly in his arms.

Briggins reached down a hand to help them up off the floor. "Come on, we need to get you two checked out by a doctor."

"We're fine," Dante said.

"All right, if you're sure, we'll get you to the field office for debriefing. I'll get someone to take Miss Kingston's statement and drive her home."

"She's staying with me," Dante said possessively. He hadn't asked her, he just knew he never wanted to let her go and he wasn't ready to let her out of his sight. Elle leaned her head against his shoulder and wrapped an arm around his waist. Obviously she felt the same way.

Many hours later—after the bomb squad had shown up to take away the bomb Elle had defused, after the crime scene team had finished collecting evidence, after they'd sat through a debriefing with Briggins—they were finally free to go.

It was midnight as Dante and Elle stood on the steps of the FBI field-office building looking into each other's eyes. "I'm sorry about Mark," he said.

"I am, too." Elle nodded. "He had so much to offer the world. I don't know why he chose the wrong path."

"Greed."

"I suppose."

"You okay."

"Uh-huh."

Dante awkwardly shifted his weight, not knowing what else to do or what to say, uncertain how much Mark's death had affected her. He didn't want to leave her side, but he didn't want to crowd her. He wasn't used to this intimacy stuff. Didn't know when to push, when to back off.

"Will I see you tomorrow?"

"Dante…" Her eyes were wide and her lip was trembling.

"Yes?"

"I don't want to be alone."

His heart leaped. "Would you like to go to my place?"

Her smile was slight but heartfelt. "I thought you'd never ask."

DANTE'S APARTMENT was much like the man. Minimal furniture. Spotless. No pictures on the wall. He had not made this place a home.

It made her feel sad.

But why would he decorate? He was an undercover FBI agent who worked at Quantico. He probably would be leaving Austin now that his assignment was over. She didn't want to think about that now. All she wanted was to be in his arms again.

"You're shaking," he said.

Was she?

"Are you cold?"

She shook her head.

"Shock," he told her. "Briggins was right. I should have made sure you got checked out at the hospital. You took a blow to the head. You could have a concussion."

She raised a hand to finger the knot at her temple. It ached, but that wasn't why she felt so unsettled. "I don't have a concussion. I'm fine."

"You've been through a big trauma today."

"You're used to this kind of thing, I suppose."

"Not really," he said. "I've been with the FBI for four years, but only as a surgeon. I give new faces to people in the witness protection program."

"My instincts told me you were law enforcement," she said. "Because of my family."

"You're perceptive."

They stood in his sterile white kitchen that she doubted he'd ever cooked in, with their eyes pinned on each other.

She studied his face, which now seemed so impossibly dear. Studied his rugged, angular lips and his dark, observant eyes. Her gaze dropped to his right hand, bandaged up tight after his run-in with the hostage-taking patient hopped up on Rapture. Then she shifted her gaze to his left hand, his wrist encircled with the barbwire tattoo.

Her heart fluttered restlessly.

"You saved our lives today," he said. "I want to thank you for that."

"I do what I can," she smiled, trying to make a joke of it, trying to belie the serious feelings knocking against her heart.

Darn if Dante's dark brown stoic eyes weren't misted with a light dusting of tears.

"When Gambezi dragged you into the lab, I thought…" His words caught in his throat. "Oh God, Elle, I thought I'd lost you forever."

She stretched out her arm. "What are you doing standing halfway across the room?"

He rushed to her then, wrapped his arms around her and kissed her lips, which were desperately hungering for him.

It was the sweetest, most gentle kiss he'd ever given her. A kiss that said *I love you* all on its own. So what if the man couldn't tell her? His lips didn't lie. She would rather have a man like Dante who couldn't say the words but meant them with all his heart, than a man like Mark who said the words when he didn't mean them.

After a few minutes, Dante pulled back and peered deeply into her eyes. He was so handsome with his hair falling across his forehead instead of brushed back like he normally wore it. His gaze tracked over her body, taking in her totally unattractive hospital scrubs, staring at her as if she were wearing the finest Victoria's Secret lingerie that money could buy.

"What?" she said. "Do I have something on my face?"

"You are truly beautiful, Elle, both inside and out," he said. "I still can't believe how close we came to…"

"It's okay," she said. "Everything turned out all right."

"It could have gone so wrong."

"It didn't. We've been given a second chance." She pushed an index finger into the cleft of his chin. "Let's not waste it."

He took her right hand with his left, folded his fingers around it and pressed their joined hands against his chest. She could feel his heart beating a ragged rhythm beneath his skin.

"What's changed?" she asked.

"I realized that no matter how much I try to be perfect and not make a mistake that it can never happen. I've made so many mistakes, Elle."

"Dante, we both have."

"We've got a lot to talk about," he said. "There are things about me that you need to know before we take this any further."

"It can wait," she said. "I'm not going anywhere."

His eyes filled with silent gratitude. "Elle," he whispered and brushed his lips against her forehead. "My sweet Elle."

*My sweet Elle.*

He said it as if he meant it. As if he truly considered her to be his.

She could barely comprehend all that had happened, all the changes that had occurred in Dante in such a short amount of time. Gone was his cool, controlled demeanor. For the first time, he was letting her see the real Dante buried beneath the guarded surface. Tender, vulnerable, yearning for something he was afraid to wish for. She felt as if he'd given her the greatest gift in the world.

"Take me to bed, Dante," she said.

Desire glazed his eyes. He let go of her hand to cup her chin in his palm. "You need to rest," he said. "And you need time to process what happened to Mark. I know you think you're over him, but you were married to the man and now he's dead. You need to grieve."

His thumb brushed her bottom lip and she shivered against him. "Dante," she whispered softly. "Dante."

He leaned in close. "Yes."

Elle's heart beat like a wild thing inside of her chest. If he didn't kiss her again she would come undone. He had to kiss her. He was the only solid thing she could depend on, the only sure thing in her life at this moment.

"Dante."

"Elle."

His gaze searched her face and she searched his. Looking into his eyes she forgot about bombs and drugs and crazy patients and dangerous criminals and a dead ex-husband.

Dante had so many layers to his personality that she had yet to peel back, so many things about him she did not know. The corners of his mouth were hard-lined and un-yielding, but she knew his lips were soft. The contradictions in him excited her. She felt as if she was teetering on some great chasm and he was the glorious abyss.

With a groan, he pulled her closer and his mouth was on hers, tasting of nervousness and uncertainty.

Who was he trying to kid? she wondered.

He was as vulnerable as she was, maybe even more so. He had no family to turn to, no one to rely on, and today, he'd lost an old friend.

His mouth was hungry, searching, promising her that they could wipe the slate clean and make a fresh start.

Ah yes, this was what she craved. Sexual oblivion.

His hands were at her back, smoothly sliding down her spine. She arched into him.

Trust. Acceptance. Redemption.

She began to undress them both and he let her.

First she loosened his tie and tossed it over the back of the kitchen chair. Then came his jacket. After that, she undid the buttons on his shirt. Freeing him from the tyranny of his clothing.

She stripped her scrub top over her head and unhooked her bra so that they were both naked from the waist up.

Dante groaned low in his throat like a jungle cat at the sight of her breasts. He dipped his head to kiss one achy breast and then the other before he would let her finish undressing them. A hot flush of pleasure flooded her body at the sensation of his warm, moist mouth gently suckling her pert nipple.

Elle kicked off her shoes and so did Dante. They grinned at each other as they both got an inch shorter.

Then she reached for his belt and slowly, seductively un-
buckled it and pulled it through the loops. It made a
whispery slithering noise.

Her fingers teased his zipper and she felt his already
erect penis get even stiffer.

She shucked off his pants and underwear in one smooth
motion, peeled off his socks and then stood up to give him
an impish come-hither grin.

"My turn," he said, and knelt in front of her, pulling her
scrubs down her hips to her ankles.

She kicked out of them.

He kissed her navel and sent a shock of awareness an-
gling down deep in her crotch. She fisted her fingers in his
hair and gasped when he took her white panties between
his teeth and pulled them down the length of her legs.

She quivered against him and he buried his face in the
triangle of her hair.

"You are so beautiful." He breathed in a reverential sigh.

When he said it, she did feel beautiful. The sweetness
of the moment made her heart ache.

"This way," he said, taking her hand in his and leading
her into his bedroom.

Dante lay down on the bed and pulled her gently on top
of him, holding her close, smiling into her face. She curled
against him. He made her feel important, needed. Trusted.

He touched his lips to hers.

And then time spun away from them. It ceased to exist
in the midst of this incredible sense of wonder.

They'd almost died today, but they had survived. The
power of it was undeniable and that bond cemented for them.

Elle had thought she wanted nothing but sex with
Dante, but this was so much better. She'd thought that
Dante was nothing more than a way to get her divorce out

of her system, but she'd been so wrong. She wanted more. Needed more from him.

They caressed each other tenderly with lingering fingers, finding the exquisite spots that made each other smile and squirm with delight.

"Hold up your left hand," he said.

She did as he asked.

He pressed the palm of his own left hand against hers. Elle felt the tingling flow of electricity from him to her and back again.

Love. True love. Born of something beyond them both, not simply from need or longing or desire. This was more.

This was true rapture, not a drug, not a fantasy, but love. Real, honest and undying love. There was no other word for the sensation she was feeling.

Dante's lips slid down her throat to her breast again. He kissed each nipple, then after a time, began to suckle them with his mouth as his hand crept to the apex between her legs. Gently he eased her legs apart and began to do amazing things with his fingers, finding tantalizing spots she never knew existed.

He kept touching her and tenderly nibbling her nipples, and the next thing she knew she was moaning softly, lost in bliss.

Slowly he trailed both his fingers and lips down her inner thighs to her feet. The tickly sensation had her laughing. She watched transfixed as Dante kissed each toe separately, and then traced his tongue in small circles around her instep.

"You taste so good," he murmured.

Elle trembled at his touch.

Shifting his position, Dante propped himself on his elbow and looked down at her. His eyes shining with an emotion she'd never seen on his face.

She prayed he was feeling it, too—this overwhelming sensation of completeness and belonging.

Abruptly, self-doubt filled her.

What if he didn't? What if she was feeling this alone? Terrified that she had read everything wrong, Elle rolled away from him, sat up straight and pulled the covers over her.

"Elle?"

"Uh-huh?"

"Are you all right?" Dante sat up, as well, and draped his bandaged hand over his knee.

"Um, sure."

"What's wrong?" Gently he grabbed one corner of the sheet she held to her breasts and tugged at it. "Why are you hiding from me?"

Elle clung to the plain white cotton sheet. Curled both fists around it. Lifted it to her chin. As a barrier it wasn't much, but she felt so naked.

So exposed.

"What's the matter?" he cooed. "Did I make a misstep? Touch the wrong place? Use too much pressure?" His voice lowered. "Did I hurt you somehow?"

"I can't...I don't..." she said, avoiding looking at him.

"I'm listening."

"I'm scared," she confessed. "I'm feeling things that I'm not used to feeling."

"Me, too, sweetheart," he said. "And I'm just as scared as you are."

"Really?"

"I've never been here before. Never felt like this," Dante admitted.

She dropped the sheet and let it fall below her breasts. She peered up from behind a thick strand of hair that had fallen across her face. "Is your heart racing as fast as mine?"

Tentatively he took her hand and pressed it against his chest. His pulse was thundering.

"See what you do to me, Elle?"

"Is your stomach all quivery?"

"Like Jell-o."

"And it's hard to breathe?"

"I'm ready to order an oxygen tank."

"What does it mean?"

"I think it means we've got it bad."

"Is it serious, doctor?" she teased.

"I'm afraid we've got a terminal case."

She stared at him and her heartbeat stalled. "A terminal case of what?"

"Love," he said and then his mouth came down hard on hers and she tasted the yearning on his lips, the urgency of his body.

Her own body was just as eager, just as frantic. Around him, she felt womanly, desirable.

His hands moved down her shoulders and her body came alive with pleasure. She whimpered helplessly into his mouth as he kissed her.

"That's right, sweetheart, lie back, relax and let me pleasure you," he urged, giving her permission to do the one thing she'd never been able to do.

Until now.

Until Dante.

Surrendering to the moment, she gave up trying to please everyone except herself. She lay back, relaxed and let Dante have his way with her.

THIS WAS WHAT HE'D BEEN missing his entire life.

Love. Real and solid and lasting.

He'd been closed off for so long. Shut down from his

emotions. Avoiding relationships, eschewing commitment. Trying to fix what was wrong with him by being perfect. By clinging to the illusion that if he was just good enough then everything would be okay. It was a crippling belief and it had kept him from making those close connections.

Even with Leeza. He'd been too hard on her, he recognized now. Had expected too much. That's why she hadn't come to him when she was in trouble. She was afraid of disappointing him. He vowed never to make Elle feel that way. He wanted her to always feel as if she could come to him and he wouldn't judge her.

Firmly she stroked his forearm with her thumb and index finger, tickling him so lightly his arm hairs lifted. She pressed her naked body against his until he could feel her everywhere. Then she lowered her head and licked his skin. With each bold stroke of her tongue, she dared him to resist her, challenging him to deny what they both wanted so desperately. Her lips taunted, punishing him for provoking her.

Even through the haze of their mind-soaking arousal, there was no denying that she pushed him to levels he'd never before experienced. Intensity rose off her like heat off the desert sand.

His biceps quivered beneath her fingertips. His hips pressed into her as if he would never let her up off his bed.

Desire ignited and surged through his shaft, snatching him up in a swell of passion.

She kept kissing his chest, his collarbone, his nipples, doing these absolutely incredible things with her tongue.

His erection ached, heavy and taut. He was eager to feel the caress of her fingers down there. Hungry to construct memories he would never forget. He wanted to remember this night forever. The first time he'd fallen in love. He intended it to be the last.

For better or for worse, he was going to make Elle Kingston his.

"Wait," he said and wriggled away from her. "Before we go any further we need to talk."

"Dante, you're torturing me."

"I want you, too, but I've kept myself closed off for so long. I want you to know me. The real me. No undercover lies. No walls between us."

She sat up against the headboard then, dragging the sheet up to cover her breasts. There was no mistaking the happy little smile curling her lips. "Are you sure?"

"I've never been surer of anything in my life."

But even though he was sure, this was difficult. Life had taught him to be guarded. His mother's abandonment, his father's abuse, Leeza's death—all stones in the wall of his emotional fortress. He was going to have to knock it all down. The thought left him feeling vulnerable and weak-kneed.

"I'm listening," she encouraged.

Dante hesitated. Emotional intimacy took courage. Was he ready? What if she swallowed him up? What if he forgot who he was?

*Stall tactics. You're just scared.*

He took a deep breath and began, "I never had a family like yours, Elle. I don't have any idea how to love."

"Yes, you do," she cooed and traced a finger over his heart. "It's innate inside you. Inside here. The hard part is letting it out. I promise not to hurt you, Dante. You truly can trust me."

His sinuses ached and he felt himself blinking. He wasn't crying. He was a tough guy, and tough guys didn't cry. But deep down inside of him was that kid who'd been left to fend for himself, to find his own way in the world.

He took a deep breath and very slowly began to tell her everything. About his parents, about Leeza, about the reason he'd joined the FBI.

She listened without commenting, occasionally clicking her tongue in sympathy, or smiling sadly or quietly stoking his cheek with her index finger. The woman made him feel safe in a way he had never felt. It was scary, but it was wonderful, too.

When he finished, it seemed as if a giant boulder had been rolled off his chest. The wall was down and Elle had walked right in.

"Thank you," she said, "for telling me all that. And from now on, it's a brand-new start." Then she leaned over and playfully kissed the tip of his nose before moving down to his mouth.

While her mouth was kissing, her fingers were busy, as well, tracing and stroking and kneading. Dante dissolved into a steamy puddle of desperate lust, while the most masculine part of his anatomy hardened to granite under her touch.

She straddled him, planting a knee on either side of his waist. The head of his penis jutted firmly against her bottom.

Dante could not have prevented his hips from arching upward if Briggins had burst into the room to announce that they had Gambezi in custody.

While she planted more erotic love bites along his neck, she ground her pelvis against his waist in undulating movements that let him know exactly how much she wanted him. Dante was overwhelmed.

She kept up the steady circle, rubbing her sex over his pelvis, teasing his throbbing erection but not letting him in just yet. He let her play. Enjoyed the game. Before, he would not have been able to lie like this and let her take control. He would have had to be in charge. But he knew now if their relationship was going to work, the power had to be shared. And he wanted this to work more than he wanted to breathe. So he let her have her fun, and in turn, his own arousal escalated, becoming more than he ever imagined it could be.

Dante splayed a hand to her chest, felt the wild pounding of her restless heart.

She was as hungry for him as he was for her, and the love in her eyes was burning bright.

For him.

*I'm responsible for this,* he thought in amazement. *She wants me. She's in love with me.*

He couldn't get over how gorgeous she looked—sparkling blue eyes, perky breasts, beautiful red hair tumbling about her shoulders, the faintest dusting of freckles across the bridge of her nose—or how soft she felt. This was love of the most delicious kind. With Elle, he felt as if he could at last lay down his arms and be who he was always meant to be.

Her eyes were open wide and she was staring at him as if he was the most incredible thing she had ever seen. The look sent a fresh surge of blood throbbing through his shaft. He felt the hot, rapid rise of it.

"Dante," she whispered. "Oh, Dante. I love how hard you are for me."

"No Rapture needed," he said lightly.

"What do you mean?" she asked. "This is total rapture."

"All my life, I've tried to be strong. I always fell far too short. But then you came along and I stopped trying to take control of everything, and now, when I look into your eyes and see the way that you see me, I feel in control of my life at last."

"Dante," she whispered. "That's the sweetest thing anyone has ever said to me."

The urgent thrust of their passion had slipped a bit, but in its place came a softer, easier kind of desire. He still craved her with an undeniable need, but there was something much deeper here.

He pulled her down and kissed her again, swallowing the giddy giggle in her throat. He tasted her joy on his tongue.

They moved in perfect union, their bodies pressed close together, smoothly, in tandem.

A heated calm seeped through his body as he experienced a blissful sense of homecoming. A wondrous peace unlike anything he'd ever known. He understood the mystery of creation, recognized the cosmic connection between them. They were one soul, one entity. Her eyes latched onto his and he could not look away. Did not want to look away.

They climaxed together like that, locked in each other's embrace.

Elle collapsed against his chest, their bodies slick with the aftersheen of extraordinary lovemaking. Dante wrapped his arms around her and buried his face in her hair, inhaled the sweet, honest scent of her, pressed his palms to the back of her head and cradled her tightly.

He'd never felt as vulnerable as he did in this moment and yet, he'd never felt more invincible.

This wasn't mere lust he felt, it wasn't just love—they were bonded for life. They were connected on an eternal level that mistakes and heartaches could not destroy. They were two halves of a single beating heart.

# *Epilogue*

MOST OF THE STAFF at Confidential Rejuvenations thought the danger was over once Mark Lawson's illegal drug operation had been destroyed. Most of them foolishly thought they were safe. Most of them never guessed that, inside the confines of those peaceful vine-covered walls, one of their own was methodically plotting to systemically destroy the place they loved. The incident had been nothing more than a delightfully unexpected bonus. The brutal murder of one of the owners had thrown the place into turmoil.

*Nicely done, Lawson. The staff will be totally unprepared for what's coming next.*

So far the attacks had been minor. A leak to the tabloid paparazzi, a small kitchen fire, a few items stolen, a transformer knocked out, a generator tampered with, but that was just the beginning. Things were about to get hot.

*Strap yourself in, folks.* From here on out, the ride was going to get very bumpy indeed.

For there was no sweeter dish than revenge. No satisfaction so great as getting even with those who'd lied and deceived and hidden the truth. No obsession as compelling as payback.

The arrogant, know-it-all staff had to be punished. Every last one of them.

And first on the list—Dr. Vanessa Rodriquez.

The bitch.

\* \* \* \* \*

*Don't miss SECRET SEDUCTION, the second compelling story in the PERFECT ANATOMY series, coming August 2008!*

*The editors at Harlequin Blaze have never been afraid to
push the limits—tempting readers with the forbidden,
whetting their appetites with a wide variety of story lines.
But now we're breaking the final barrier—the time barrier.*

*In July, watch for BOUND TO PLEASE
by fan favorite Hope Tarr, Harlequin Blaze's
first ever historical romance—a story that's
truly Blaze-worthy in every sense.*

*Here's a sneak peek...*

Brianna stretched out beside Ewan, languid as a cat, and promptly fell asleep. Midday sunshine streamed into the chamber, bathing her lovely, long-limbed body in golden light, the sea-scented breeze wafting inside to dry the damp red-gold tendrils curling about her flushed face. Propping himself up on one elbow, Ewan slid his gaze over her. She looked beautiful and whole, satisfied and sated, and altogether happier than he had so far seen her. A slight smile curved her beautiful lips as though she must be in the midst of a lovely dream. She'd molded her lush, lovely body to his and laid her head in the curve of his shoulder and settled in to sleep beside him. For the longest while he lay there turned toward her, content to watch her sleep, at near perfect peace.

Not wholly perfect, for she had yet to answer his marriage proposal. Still, she wanted to make a baby with him, and Ewan no longer viewed her plan as the travesty he once had. He wanted children—sons to carry on after him, though a bonny little daughter with flame-colored hair would be nice, too. But he also wanted more than to simply plant his seed and be on his way. He wanted to lie beside Brianna night upon night as she increased, rub soothing unguents into the swell of her belly, knead the ache from her back and make slow, gentle love to her. He wanted to hold his newly born child in his arms and look down into

Brianna's tired but radiant face and blot the perspiration from her brow and be a husband to her in every way.

He gave her a gentle nudge. "Brie?"

"Hmm?"

She rolled onto her side and he captured her against his chest. One arm wrapped about her waist, he bent to her ear and asked, "Do you think we might have just made a baby?"

Her eyes remained closed, but he felt her tense against him. "I don't know. We'll have to wait and see."

He stroked his hand over the flat plane of her belly. "You're so small and tight it's hard to imagine you increasing."

"All women increase no matter how large or small they start out. I may not grow big as a croft, but I'll be big enough, though I have hopes I may not waddle like a duck, at least not too badly."

The reference to his fair-day teasing was not lost on him. He grinned. "Brianna MacLeod grown so large she must sit still for once in her life. I'll need the proof of my own eyes to believe it."

Despite their banter, he felt his spirits dip. Assuming they were so blessed, he wouldn't have the chance to see her thus. By then he would be long gone, restored to his clan according to the sad bargain they'd struck. He opened his mouth to ask her to marry him again and then clamped it closed, not wanting to spoil the moment, but the unspoken words weighed like a millstone on his heart.

The damnable bargain they'd struck was proving to be a devil's pact indeed.

\* \* \* \* \*

*Will these two star-crossed lovers*
*find their sexily-ever-after?*
*Find out in Bound to Please by Hope Tarr,*
*available in July wherever*
*Harlequin® Blaze™ books are sold.*

## Harlequin Blaze marks new territory with its first historical novel!

For years readers have trusted the Harlequin Blaze series to entertain them with a variety of stories— Now Blaze is breaking down the final barrier— the time barrier!

Welcome to Blaze Historicals—all the sexiness you love in a Blaze novel, all the adventure of a historical romance. It's the best of both worlds!

### Don't miss the first book in this exciting new miniseries:

## BOUND TO PLEASE
### by Hope Tarr

New laird Brianna MacLeod knows she can't protect her land or her people without a man by her side. So what else can she do—she kidnaps one! Only, she doesn't expect to find herself the one enslaved....

### Available in July wherever Harlequin books are sold.

# SPECIAL EDITION™

## NEW YORK TIMES BESTSELLING AUTHOR

# DIANA PALMER

A brand-new Long, Tall Texans novel

# HEART OF STONE

Feeling unwanted and unloved, Keely returns to Jacobsville and to Boone Sinclair, a rancher troubled by his own past. Boone has always seemed reserved, but now Keely discovers a sensuality with him that quickly turns to love. Can they each see past their own scars to let love in?

*Available September 2008 wherever you buy books.*

# HIGH-SOCIETY SECRET PREGNANCY

### *Park Avenue Scandals*

Self-made millionaire Max Rolland had given
up on love until he meets socialite fundraiser
Julia Prentice. After their encounter Julia finds
herself pregnant, but a mysterious blackmailer
threatens to use this surprise pregnancy and ruin
his reputation. Max must decide whether to turn
his back on the woman carrying his child or risk
everything, including his heart....

**Don't miss the next installment of
the Park Avenue Scandals series—
*Front Page Engagement*
by Laura Wright—
coming in August 2008
from Silhouette Desire!**

**Always Powerful, Passionate and Provocative.**

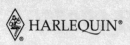

# REQUEST YOUR FREE BOOKS!

## 2 FREE NOVELS
## PLUS 2
## FREE GIFTS!

HARLEQUIN®

*Blaze*™

### Red-hot reads!

**YES!** Please send me 2 FREE Harlequin® Blaze™ novels and my 2 FREE gifts (gifts are worth about $10). After receiving them, if I don't wish to receive any more books, I can return the shipping statement marked "cancel". If I don't cancel, I will receive 6 brand-new novels every month and be billed just $4.24 per book in the U.S. or $4.71 per book in Canada, plus 25¢ shipping and handling per book and applicable taxes, if any*. That's a savings of 15% or more off the cover price! I understand that accepting the 2 free books and gifts places me under no obligation to buy anything. I can always return a shipment and cancel at any time. Even if I never buy another book, the two free books and gifts are mine to keep forever.

151 HDN ERVA  351 HDN ERUX

| | |
|---|---|
| Name | (PLEASE PRINT) |
| Address | Apt. # |
| City | State/Prov. | Zip/Postal Code |

Signature (if under 18, a parent or guardian must sign)

### Mail to the **Harlequin Reader Service:**
**IN U.S.A.:** P.O. Box 1867, Buffalo, NY 14240-1867
**IN CANADA:** P.O. Box 609, Fort Erie, Ontario L2A 5X3

Not valid to current subscribers of Harlequin Blaze books.

### Want to try two free books from another line?
### Call 1-800-873-8635 or visit www.morefreebooks.com.

\* Terms and prices subject to change without notice. N.Y. residents add applicable sales tax. Canadian residents will be charged applicable provincial taxes and GST. Offer not valid in Quebec. This offer is limited to one order per household. All orders subject to approval. Credit or debit balances in a customer's account(s) may be offset by any other outstanding balance owed by or to the customer. Please allow 4 to 6 weeks for delivery. Offer available while quantities last.

**Your Privacy:** Harlequin Books is committed to protecting your privacy. Our Privacy Policy is available online at www.eHarlequin.com or upon request from the Reader Service. From time to time we make our lists of customers available to reputable third parties who may have a product or service of interest to you. If you would prefer we not share your name and address, please check here. ☐

HB08R

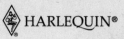

## COMING NEXT MONTH

### #405 WHAT I DID ON MY SUMMER VACATION
**Thea Divine, Debbi Rawlins, Samantha Hunter**
*A Sizzling Summer Collection*
Three single women end up with a fling worth writing about in this Blazing summer collection. Whether they spend their time in the city, in the woods or at the beach, their reports are bound to be strictly X-rated!

### #406 INCOGNITO  Kate Hoffmann
*Forbidden Fantasies*
Haven't you ever wished you could be someone else? Lily Hart has. So when she's mistaken for a promiscuous celebrity, she jumps at the chance to live out the erotic lifestyle she's always envied. After all, nobody will find out. Or will they?

### #407 BOUND TO PLEASE  Hope Tarr
*Blaze Historicals*
*Blaze marks new territory with its first historical novel!* New laird Brianna MacLeod knows she can't protect her land or her people without a man by her side. So, she kidnaps one! Only, she never expects to find herself the one enslaved....

### #408 HEATED RUSH  Leslie Kelly
*The Wrong Bed: Again and Again*
Annie Davis is in trouble. Her big family reunion is looming, and she needs a stand-in man—fast. Her solution? Bachelor number twenty at the charity bachelor auction. But there's more to her rent-a-date than meets the eye....

### #409 BED ON ARRIVAL  Kelley St. John
*The Sexth Sense*
Jenee Vicknair is keeping a wicked secret. Every night she has wild, mind-blowing sex with a perfect stranger. They never exchange words—their bodies say everything that needs to be said. If only her lover didn't vanish into thin air the moment the satisfaction was over....

### #410 FLASHPOINT  Jill Shalvis
*American Heroes: The Firefighters*
Zach Thomas might put out fires for a living, but when the sexy firefighter meets EMT Brooke O'Brian, all he wants to do is stoke her flames. Still, can Brooke count on him to take the heat if the sparks between them flare out of control?

**www.eHarlequin.com**

HBCNM0608